Finders Keepers

Roy Deering

THE ROADRUNNER PRESS
OKLAHOMA CITY, OKLAHOMA

Published by The RoadRunner Press
Oklahoma City, Oklahoma
www.TheRoadRunnerPress.com

This is a work of fiction. While the literary perceptions and insights
are based on experience, all names, characters, places, and incidents are
either products of the author's imagination or are used fictitiously.
No reference to any real person is intended or should be inferred.

First Edition December 2014
Printed in the United States of America
by Maple Press, York, Pennsylvania

This book is available for special promotions, premiums, and group sales.
For details e-mail Director of Special Sales at info@theroadrunnerpress.com.

Library of Congress Control Number: 201456131

Publisher's Cataloging-In-Publication Data
(Prepared by The Donohue Group, Inc.)
Deering, Roy.
  Finders keepers / Roy Deering. -- First edition.

    pages ; cm

  Summary: When Mr. Martin hired his son's best friend, Tomás, to clean out the old family store, he was trying to get an unsafe, dirty job done on the cheap. He never expected the boy to turn up hidden treasure. Now their deal is the talk of the town.
  Interest age level: 008-016.

  ISBN: 978-1-937054-11-3 (HC)
  ISBN: 978-1-937054-14-4 (TP)
  ISBN: 978-1-937054-13-7 (eBook)

  1. Hispanic American boys--Juvenile fiction. 2. Stores, Retail--Juvenile fiction. 3. Treasure troves--Juvenile fiction. 4. Racism--Juvenile fiction. 5. Boys--Fiction. 6. Hispanic Americans--Fiction. 7. Stores, Retail--Fiction. 8. Buried treasure--Fiction. 9. Racism--Fiction. I. Title.

PZ7.D447 Fi 2014
[Fic]   2014956131

10 9 8 7 6 5 4 3 2 1

*This book is dedicated to my family,
who have followed me from one end of the
earth to the other without complaint.
I love you all more than you could ever understand.
Thanks for never giving up on me.*

Finders Keepers

Chapter 1

Tomás Martinez adjusted his baseball cap and turned the corner toward the old Martin Five & Dime on West Main Street.

It was just after nine in the morning, but the temperature on the sign at the South Texas Bank of San Moreno already read ninety-two degrees. It was going to be a sizzler. Tomás patted his back pockets to make sure he still had his work gloves and flashlight. *Check. Check.* The job was going to be brutal enough what with the Texas heat and humidity without arriving ill prepared.

But if I finish by four o'clock, I'll be fifty dollars richer, and that will help mother.

Since his father had gone to prison six months ago, Tomás's mom had struggled to keep food on the table, but not from a lack of trying. Once again this morning she had been up long before dawn, on the way to her job as a housekeeper for the Days Inn out by the highway north of town. She was working twelve to fourteen hours a day to earn as much overtime as possible. It was hard on her, and hard on Tomás to see her doing it.

But what other choice do we have? Tomás shook his head. *No point in rehashing what can't be changed.*

He cupped his hands against the front window of the old store and peered inside. Dusty display shelves lay scattered about and chunks of insulation carpeted the floor like dirty pink snow. Mr. Martin had told him no one had been inside the store for more than five years, and he had warned Tomás he should be prepared to find rat nests among the debris.

Terrific. He hated rats.

He also had to hurry. If he didn't finish by four, he would not get paid. He turned the key in the lock and pushed open the old door, waiting for his eyes to adjust to the darkness. The musty stench of dirt and mildew was overpowering at first, but after a few minutes he was almost able to ignore the horrible smell. *Almost.* He heaved a heavy sigh, pulled on his work gloves, and began dragging trash out to the big blue dumpster in front of the building.

*****

By the time the clock at the First Baptist Church chimed the noon hour, Tomás had cleared a path from the front door to the main checkout counter of the old store. His face was covered with grime and his shirt was damp with sweat. The only good news was that so far no rat had shown itself.

He looked around. He was going to have to pick up the pace. Mr. Martin had made it very clear that if the building was not cleared out by day's end, Tomás would not be getting paid. *Wouldn't that be a drag—can't think of anything worse than working all day in a hot, smelly rat-infested building, except working all day in a hot, smelly rat-infested building for free!*

Tomás was excited about the prospect of making fifty dollars to help his mom, but he was also keeping an eye out for something for himself. Mr. Martin had told him he could keep anything he found in the old store. So far, other than a broken cash register and a few pieces of shelving he thought his mother might use, he hadn't found anything he wanted. But he hadn't given up hope.

Tomás knew the store's toy department had once been legendary among the children of San Moreno, though he himself had never been inside. Mr. Martin's father had opened the Five & Dime back in 1949, and everyone within fifty miles of town shopped there until the Walmart arrived out by the highway fifteen years ago. Old Mr. Martin finally closed the store, and within a year he was dead from a heart attack. *Looks like no one has been in here since the old man died.*

From the outside, the store still looked in pretty good shape, but inside the building was a disaster, a stinky, filthy

3

disaster. Someone had vandalized the place about a year ago; Tomás knew Mr. Martin had publicly blamed the damage on "those Mexican kids." It was possible whoever had vandalized the building was Hispanic, but Tomás also knew everything bad that happened in town was blamed on his people, even if they had nothing to do with it.

He poked behind the checkout counter where customers had once paid for their purchases. A thick layer of dust covered the counter's surface, but luckily he didn't see a lot of trash behind it to remove. He squeezed between the wall and the counter trying to make sure, catching his T-shirt on a nail in the process. He winced as he heard his sleeve tear.

Angry at putting a hole in his T-shirt, Tomás attacked the guilty nail with a scrap of metal. As he pried the nail loose, the paneling began to pull away from the wall, exposing a larger-than-expected empty space behind it. *That's strange*—was Tomás's first thought. His second thought made him shiver. *Perfect spot for a rat nest.*

He dropped the piece of metal and tried to push the faded brown paneling back into place. The panel would have none of it. It popped right back out as soon as Tomás let go. Tomás realized he had no choice—Mr. Martin would never pay him if the loose paneling were left behind. He grabbed the panel and pulled hard, ripping the rest of the four-foot section free from the studs. Nothing moved. Tomás breathed a sigh of relief.

With his fear of waking a nest of rats gone, at least for the moment, Tomás had to admit he found the hole curious. It looked to be a dark crawl space about four feet high and three feet wide. It extended back several feet into the dark.

Tomás grabbed his flashlight off the counter and shined it into the bowels of the wall. The beam glanced off something. Tomás directed the light to that spot.

What was that by the back wall?

If his eyes weren't deceiving him, the dark recess held a stack of boxes wrapped in thick plastic, each box about two feet square and covered in a layer of dust.

Tomás now realized the hole was actually some kind of special storage place, like a safe but with only three sides and a top and bottom. The inside lining of the hole was hard, maybe concrete or plaster. As for the boxes, it looked like there were six of them—and they were just out of his reach.

Tomás did not even hesitate.

He dropped to his knees and crawled into the opening—all worries about rats or other varmints gone. Once inside, he pointed his flashlight at the box closest to him and wiped away a swath of the thick dust that covered it.

Using the beam of the flashlight, he made out the word "Topps" through two layers of thick plastic wrap.

That's when he dropped the flashlight.

Chapter 2

Sam Coberly was looking for his car keys when he heard banging on the glass front door of his office. Sam always seemed to be looking for his keys. He moved across the office, still glancing about for them while the banging continued.

"Okay!" he shouted through the glass. "I'm coming. Hold your horses."

When he opened the door, two small boys looked up at him from under dirty baseball caps. Behind them was a beat up red wagon, piled high with cardboard boxes covered in what looked like plastic wrap.

"Mr. Coberly?" the shorter of the two boys asked.

"Yeah, I'm Sam."

"I found something, and I think I might need a lawyer," said the boy.

Sam Coberly smiled and stepped back, holding open the door.

"Come on in, gentlemen," he said. "My door's always open to men in trouble."

*****

Ten minutes later the six still dusty plastic-wrapped cardboard boxes sat on a long wooden conference table in the downtown offices of Samuel J. Coberly, Attorney at Law. Tomás and another boy sat side by side in matching leather chairs in front of the lawyer's desk. Sam Coberly sat back in his chair and looked quizzically at the boys.

"So you found these cards, or what you think are baseball cards, inside the old Martin store?"

"That's right, Mr. Coberly," Tomás said. "They were inside the wall, wrapped in plastic, and all covered with dust just like they are now."

Coberly stood slowly, a smile spreading across his face. A small man with snow-white hair, he was seventy-three years old and not particularly well liked by a certain faction of residents of San Moreno. For whatever reason, however, he was the attorney local Hispanics called when they had legal problems. From disputes with landlords to problems with local law enforcement officers, the town's Mexican-American residents knew they could trust Sam to represent them without prejudice.

"So, just out of curiosity, what time was it when you found these boxes?" Coberly asked.

7

Tomás thought for a minute. He had been so busy trying to finish cleaning out the building by his deadline and so excited about finding the boxes he had lost all track of time.

"I think it was a little after noon. I remember hearing the church bells."

Coberly glanced at the old grandfather clock across the room.

"It's a little after five now," he said. "Where in heaven's name did you keep these boxes for almost four hours while you finished cleaning out that building?"

"They were out on the sidewalk," Tomás said.

"Do you think maybe it could have been a little unwise to just leave them outside on the sidewalk for three or four hours where anybody could walk up and take them?" Coberly asked.

"I didn't have anyplace else to put them," Tomás said. "And the mayor is always saying San Moreno is the kind of small town where nobody locks the front door, so I figured the sidewalk was probably safe, too."

Mr. Coberly chuckled. He had heard the mayor make the very same claim more than once.

"I didn't know what else to do, Mr. Coberly," Tomás said. "I had to finish cleaning the building or Mr. Martin wouldn't pay me. I just did what I had to do to get the job done, and I figured I'd get to the boxes when I finished."

Mr. Coberly leaned forward, smiling. "You can call me Sam."

With that, Coberly leaned back in his big leather chair,

clasped his hands, and began to twirl his thumbs, a habit of his when things were getting interesting and one annoyingly familiar to his fellow barristers.

Tomás visibly relaxed a little. His quiet buddy, however, remained perched on the end of his chair in a state of high alert.

"And you're sure he told you that you could keep *anything* you found inside the building when he asked you to clean it?"

"Yes, sir," Tomás answered. "That's what he said. I never even asked. He just said, 'Clean it out. I want everything gone, and you can keep anything you want that you find in there as sort of a bonus.' "

"You're positive that's what he said?"

"He said he'd pay me fifty dollars to clean out the store, but that if I left anything in there, he wouldn't pay me. That's when he told me I could keep anything I found in there that I wanted, so long as I got it out of the building," Tomás said. "Tommy heard him say it. That's why I brought him with me."

Coberly looked across at Tommy Martin, the blond boy about to fall out of the leather chair directly to Tomás's right.

"Is that true, Tommy? Did your father tell him that?"

"Yes, sir," Tommy said quietly. "He said, 'If there's anything you find in that old building that you want, you can keep it. Just get it out of the building.' "

This was news enough to get Coberly out of his chair and from behind his desk. He came to rest on the edge of the desk facing the boys. He put a finger to his lips as if he had just thought of something important.

"Are you sure he didn't say you could keep any 'junk' you found that you wanted, or that you could have anything you found that was of no value, or trash?"

Tomás and Tommy answered in unison: "That's not what he said. We're sure."

Coberly clapped his hands together. "Good," he said.

He turned his gaze to Tomás, a wide smile playing on his face.

"What you and Mr. Martin did was enter into a contract, and you've held up your end of the bargain. Now we'll make sure Mr. Martin keeps his," Coberly said.

"Contract? But I never signed anything," Tomás said, looking uncertain again.

"Doesn't matter," Coberly said. "An agreement reached by words between two parties—known as a verbal contract—is just as strong, even if one of those parties happens to be a twelve-year-old."

Tomás considered that for a moment.

"But what if Mr. Martin says he never told me that, or that I misunderstood what he said?"

Coberly looked at Tommy, who suddenly seemed uncomfortable. "That's where young Mr. Martin comes in."

Tommy gulped, realizing where Coberly was headed. Suddenly, Sam Coberly stood.

"I'm starving," he said. "Let me make a phone call, then I'll take you boys somewhere and get us all a hamburger. Would that be okay?"

Chapter 3

Ninety minutes later, they were back in Sam's office, but a fourth person had joined them. The newcomer was a man, much younger than Sam, dressed in what looked to be a very expensive suit.

The man in the suit looked across the table at Tomás.

"Are you a baseball fan?"

"Sure," Tomás said. "Isn't everybody?"

"Son, have you ever heard of Mickey Mantle?"

"Sure. Who hasn't?"

"Hall of Fame center fielder for the New York Yankees, right?"

"Yes, sir."

"Did you know his first baseball card was issued in 1951, more than sixty years ago?"

Tomás seemed confused.

"No, sir. I'm no baseball expert. Why are you telling me this?"

"Tomás, the six boxes you found sealed up in that little crawl space contain baseball cards from a very long time ago." He looked hard at Tomás. "They're sixty years old. Do you understand what I'm trying to say?"

Tomás nodded slowly.

"You're trying to say they might be worth some money? Maybe several hundred dollars?"

The stranger looked at Coberly and laughed. Tomás sunk into his chair, embarrassed. Tommy inched back out on the edge of his chair as if he might launch himself any minute at the man in the suit for making fun of his friend, but Tommy eased back into his own chair when Sam started chuckling, too.

"You haven't told him any of this, have you?" said the man in the suit.

Coberly shook his head. "No, I thought I'd let you do the honors."

The stranger smiled and walked to the conference table where the boxes were still stacked.

"Do you know what a wax pack is?" he asked, looking back at Tomás again.

"Sure," Tomás said, heaving a sigh, relieved to know this answer. "It's a pack of baseball or football cards."

"And they sell for about how much?" the man asked.

"Three or four dollars a pack, I guess," Tomás said.

"These boxes, Tomás, are full of wax packs of very old cards that sold for a nickel each."

Tomás's face fell. "A nickel? That means they're worth barely more than a hundred dollars even if I sell them all."

He considered that for a moment then smiled.

"Well, that's less than Tommy and I thought they'd be worth, but hey, that's a hundred odd dollars my family could still use."

Once again, the stranger and Coberly looked at one another and smiled. This time, it was the lawyer who spoke.

"Tomás, those cards sold for a nickel a pack in 1952, when the Topps Company issued its first set of baseball cards. That is true. But, today, if you could even find one, it would sell for quite a bit more."

Tomás's eyes widened, and he and Tommy looked at each other excitedly.

"How much more?" Tommy asked bluntly.

"The past few years, some have sold for as much as two or three thousand dollars apiece," Coberly said. "And those were not in what they call mint condition."

He paused, waiting for a reaction, but both Tomás and Tommy sat in stunned silence.

"Not too long ago, a single wax pack sold for more than twenty-one thousand dollars at auction," Coberly said. "Twenty-one thousand dollars for a pack of baseball cards! Amazing, isn't it?"

Sam and the stranger exchanged grins. Tomás's mouth fell open, and Tommy coughed several times trying to catch his breath.

"Twenty thousand dollars? Seriously?" Tommy asked.

Coberly and the man in the suit smiled as Tomás and

Tommy tried to do the math in their heads. For several moments the only sound in the room was the ticktock of the grandfather clock. Finally Tomás stood and looked at the stranger.

"How many packs are in these boxes?"

"These 'boxes' are called cases," the man said. "There are six cases, and each of them contains twenty boxes of wax packs. Inside each of those twenty boxes are twenty-four wax packs of cards, and each wax pack could sell for twenty thousand dollars . . . or maybe more."

Tommy was trying to count on his fingers, but gave up. "That's an awful lot of money," he said.

"I think I'm going to be sick," Tomás said.

"And, you have to remember," the stranger said, pointing to the boxes on the table, "those cards you found are still in the original cases in mint condition. They've not been touched for sixty years. They're perfect, so they could easily bring substantially more than twenty thousand dollars a pack."

He watched Tomás and Tommy as they looked at each other in amazement. Truth be told, both boys now looked a little green.

"In total, that's 2,880 wax packs of cards," the man said. "And each of those is worth at least twenty thousand dollars on the market today."

Tomás had begun mumbling to himself. Tommy burst out laughing, slapping his hand on his knee in amazement.

"So exactly how much money are we talking?" Tommy asked bluntly.

"Somewhere in the neighborhood of fifty-seven to sixty million dollars, *minimum*, if you sell each wax pack separately," Coberly said. "But, what makes this even more exciting is that these are entire mint condition cases, which could greatly increase their value at auction if they were to be sold as a package—meaning all six cases being sold as one unit."

He paused for a moment, once again watching the boys' faces.

"What that means is that these cards, hidden inside that wall for nearly sixty years, could be worth a lot more than sixty million dollars, especially when the media gets hold of this story and the public hysteria hits," Coberly said. "Collectors will be coming out of the woodwork."

The man in the suit looked hard at Tomás.

"Mr. Coberly tells me you had a job to do today and you kept the cards out on the sidewalk for almost four hours while you finished, and then pulled the cards over here all the way across town in the back of an old red wagon with the help of your friend here. Is that right?"

"Yes, sir," Tomás whispered.

"Son, you do realize anybody in the world could have walked away with those cards, and you would have lost millions of dollars, just so you could earn the fifty dollars you were promised for cleaning out that old building?"

"Yes, sir," Tomás answered a little more loudly. "But I promised Mr. Martin I would finish today. And I had to be done by the time he sent Tommy to check on me."

Tommy couldn't stand it anymore.

"Sixty million dollars!" Tommy shouted, jumping up on the seat of his leather chair and doing a little dance. "Did you hear that Tomás? You're a sixty millionaire!"

Tomás stood shakily and walked to Sam's desk and lifted the phone.

"I think I need to call my mother."

Chapter 4

The first reporters started calling an hour later, prompted by a "leak" from the offices of the stranger in the dark suit. An hour after that, the first television crews rolled into town. Before dark, six television satellite trucks lined the street in front of Sam's downtown office.

By late evening, the south Texas discovery was the lead story on the three major networks and playing on a loop on CNN, ESPN, and all the cable news stations.

At Major League Baseball parks all across the country, the little boy and his "big find" were the topic of the day, even in locker rooms and dugouts—to the chagrin of some managers.

Coming off a hard-earned second win in a double-header with the Baltimore Orioles, the perennially grumpy manager of the New York Yankees was swarmed by sports reporters not for a comment on the Yankee victory but about his thoughts on the little boy in Texas who had discovered six cases of vintage baseball cards. The manager left the ballpark in disgust, though history would record that his first question upon seeing his pitching coach was, "What about these baseball cards?"

*****

Back in San Moreno, Bill Martin had not had a good day, and it was about to get worse.

Three of his illegal workers had never shown up at the job site. Because of that his crew couldn't pour the concrete foundation on Walter Brady's new six thousand-square-foot house west of town. That would cost him at least a thousand dollars, and it had forced him to put off the electrician and the plumber for three days. That would cost him even more.

Bill Martin could not afford to lose any money these days, but he especially could not afford to lose that much money in a single afternoon.

"Stupid, lazy, undependable . . ." Martin muttered under his breath. "I'd like to take the whole bunch of them and . . ."

Bill Martin was not the only south Texan to harbor ill will against Hispanics, especially illegal immigrants, but just like so many other businessmen, the success or failure of his construction business depended greatly on the same immigrant workers he held in such disdain. It was a frustrating Catch-22 situation that made him hate immigrants even more.

It infuriated Martin that so much of his daily life depended on people he could not stand. And, if that wasn't bad enough, his son had taken up with one last summer and now the two were as tight as teammates. *Of all the kids in the county for Tommy to choose as his best friend . . .*

Bill Martin took his frozen dinner out of the microwave. He had no idea where his wife and son were tonight, probably at some church function. They always seemed to be at some church function.

Steaming Mexican dinner in hand, Bill plopped into his recliner and flipped on the news. What he heard made him drop a scalding hot tamale square in his lap.

Chapter 5

Tomás peered out the office window at the mob of reporters and the rows of television cameras.

"Do we have to go out there?"

"It'll be fun," Sam said. "Think of it as your moment in the spotlight."

"I don't want a moment in the spotlight," Tomás said. "Everybody in town hates me. Everybody in Texas hates me. They all think I stole those cards."

Sam straightened his tie, looked in the mirror, and then pulled the tie off and tossed it on his desk. "Not everyone, and, after we explain what happened, everyone will see those cards are rightfully and legally yours."

Tomás looked at his mother, who stood away from the window so she could not be seen by the prying eyes of the townspeople or reporters.

Sam sensed her nervousness and tried to calm her. "Mrs. Martinez?"

"Call me Juana," she answered softly.

"Okay, Juana. It is going to be okay. They're just curious and eager to hear your side of the story. Are you ready?"

"I don't think I could ever be ready for this, but I'll go," she said.

Together the trio stepped out the door to an explosion of camera flashes and a barrage of questions. The reporters could not help noticing that the woman and boy both looked as if they would rather be anyplace else . . . and that Sam Coberly appeared to be having the time of his life.

*****

Minutes later, watching on live television across town, Bill Martin heard Sam Coberly's opening comments and threw what was left of his tamale dinner at Sam's face on the TV screen, cursing simultaneously the "little Mexican punk" who stood beside the slimy lawyer.

Meanwhile, with his hand resting assuredly on Tomás's shoulder, Sam Coberly told the world the boy's story— from Tomás's verbal agreement to clean out the building to the boy's surprise at finding the dusty boxes inside the wall to the sense of duty that wouldn't allow Tomás to leave with his treasure until his work was done.

Sam walked the media through the amazing discovery step by step. He also described the "treasure" in detail for the first time publicly, enjoying every delicious moment. He was in his element.

"We've had the boxes examined by a respected vintage baseball card expert, and he has assured us that Tomás is, in fact, the owner of six unopened cases of 1952 Topps brand baseball cards," Coberly said. "The boxes have apparently been wrapped in plastic since 1952, and have suffered absolutely no damage. That means the cards inside those cases are in mint condition, and that, as collectors know, is very important.

"Many of you already know these particular cards are the most coveted cards in the history of the hobby. It is, without a doubt, the greatest discovery in baseball card history, and the cards will likely be worth as much as sixty million dollars at auction."

The crowd was heard to give a collective gasp at that. The stakes now known, the reporters drew closer, throwing even more questions at the attorney; Sam fielded them all calmly, while smiling broadly for the cameras. Photographs would later show that Tomás looked ready to break free and run, the only thing keeping him from bolting was Sam's hand resting on the boy's shoulder.

Just when it seemed the media frenzy had reached its peak, at least for the night, Sam tossed the reporters a little more bait.

"An auction for the cards has already begun, in fact," Coberly announced. "It is being handled by the Richard Darcy Company out of Houston, and we've already received several significant bids."

Sam knew exactly what the next question would be.

"How much is the highest bid?" a reporter hollered.

Dramatically, Sam extracted a single piece of paper from the inside pocket of his blazer. He studied it for a moment, though he already knew what was written on it.

"The last one, from a New York bidder, was just under twenty million dollars," Coberly said. He paused briefly. "But we expect the bidding to continue and for the price to climb. These are, after all, the most sought-after sports memorabilia in history, and they are in pristine condition, having never been removed from their original packaging."

Suddenly, as if the mob of reporters had just realized Tomás's presence, the cameras swung in his direction. With a thousand voices shouting questions, Tomás and his mother stepped back, raising their arms to cover their eyes from the blinding lights.

"How does it feel Tomás?" "Mrs. Martinez, what will you do with sixty million dollars?" "Tomás, do you have anything to say to the world?"

Sam raised both hands to silence the mob. Tomás and his mother drew each other close, as if protecting themselves from the crowd and the flurry of questions.

"My client and his mother are extremely excited, as you might expect," Coberly said. "It has, however, been a long and tumultuous day for them, as you can imagine, and they need a few days to sort things out. But I can tell you this has been a great day for them. Thank you, folks."

A reporter from a Houston TV station pushed his way to the front of the crowd, shouting a final question:

"Mr. Coberly, have you been in contact with the man who owned the building, a Mr. Bill Martin? Have you spoken with Mr. Martin?"

Sam stood looking at the cameras for nearly five seconds before answering.

"No, we have not heard from Mr. Martin. I expect that to change in the near future," he added.

What Sam did not know was that encounter had just been delayed a little more. Mr. Martin was incommunicado, busy picking up the pieces of what remained of the cell phone he had just thrown against his living room wall.

*****

Thirty minutes later, when Tommy and his mother returned home, Bill Martin met them at the door with a hard look on his face. Behind him bits and pieces of his phone still lay scattered across the living room floor—forgotten for now in his angry eagerness to question his son about the baseball cards.

"So you knew about this all day? And you said nothing to me?"

Tommy had dreaded this moment since Tomás had first shown him the six boxes of cards at the store. He did not want to answer his father, but had no choice.

"Yes, sir. I knew."

"May I ask why you didn't think it was necessary to tell me about sixty million dollars worth of rare baseball cards your little Mexican friend found in my building?"

Tommy saw no reason to lie. It couldn't possibly get any worse. "I didn't know they would be worth that much money at first," he said. "Then, when I found out, I knew you'd be really mad, so I didn't know what to do."

"Mad?" Bill Martin nearly choked. "You thought it would make me mad?" He was pacing furiously now in front of the couch where Tommy sat.

"Mad is when you have a flat tire in the rain, or when your phone rings at three in the morning and it's a wrong number," he said, his voice getting louder. "Those are things that make me mad. This is not mad. This is something way beyond mad, Tommy, something I can't even begin to describe."

He stopped now, standing directly in front of Tommy until his son looked him in the eye.

"Do you realize your little friend could cost us sixty . . . million . . . dollars? Do you? Do you have any idea how much money that is?"

Tommy shook his head silently. And he didn't. He and Tomás had been as excited as two twelve-year-old boys could be when they had thought the cards might be worth a hundred bucks. The number of zeros Mr. Coberly, his dad, and the man in the suit were talking about now was more than Tommy could comprehend. He had tried to explain that to his mom. She had seemed to understand. But he understood why she didn't dare say anything now. It would only make his dad madder.

"We're talking big money," Bill Martin said angrily. "Sixty million at least, and probably a lot more before it

25

is all over, from what I hear. Some people say it could end up being seventy million, or even more. Can you begin to understand that, Tommy? Seventy million dollars!"

His father was screaming at him now.

"Bill, calm down," said Tommy's mother. "You're going to have a heart attack. And you're scaring Tommy."

"This is between me and Tommy," Bill retorted.

With a look of apology at her son, Tommy's mother threw up her hands and left the room, unsure what to do to return peace to her family.

Still Tommy sat silently. He had been wrong. It *could* get worse . . . and somehow he knew he hadn't seen the worst of it yet.

Bill Martin plopped back into his recliner, pressing his fingers into his forehead to try and fight off what was fast becoming a crushing headache.

"Tommy," he said softly. "My company isn't doing so great. You know that, don't you?"

"Yes, sir," Tommy said.

"Do you realize what seventy million dollars—or even one million dollars—could mean for us?"

"It would mean you wouldn't have to work anymore," Tommy said.

"That's true," his father said. "But there's a lot more to it. It would also mean we could pay what I owe the bank and later send you to college, too."

Tommy couldn't hold back anymore, although he knew what he had to say was only going to make his father more upset.

"Dad, it's not our money. They're not our cards."

Bill Martin's hands slowly slid from his face, and he stared at his son with fire in his eyes.

"What makes you say that?" he asked slowly. "You don't really believe his story about how I told him he could keep whatever he found, do you?"

"But you did say that, Dad," Tommy said. "And I know because I was sitting right there in the pickup beside you when you said it."

With that Tommy sent himself straight to bed.

Chapter 6

Tommy peeked nervously around the building, taking in what he could see with one eye—the rest of his face hidden behind the corner of the brick wall. He thought he counted five people, but however many there were, none of them noticed him.

A woman and a little girl, the latter about five years old, exited a blue Dodge minivan and started up the sidewalk. Neither of them looked in Tommy's direction.

Two teenagers—a boy and a girl—sat cross-legged on a blanket in the shade of an old oak tree. The twosome laughed quietly at a private joke and paid no attention to Tommy as he stepped around the corner and eased toward the front door of the San Moreno Public Library.

Tomás was waiting for him inside, sitting with his back to the door. He, too, was trying not to be recognized.

Tommy slid into a chair next to where his best friend was perched in front of a computer.

"I wonder if any reporters saw us," Tomás said, glancing around suspiciously. "I can't go outside without a hundred people following me, yelling questions at me, and taking my picture. This has gotten crazy."

Tommy nodded. "I know what you mean," he said. "My mom had reporters follow her to the grocery store. We even had some people from a television station trying to interview members of our church. It's wild."

Tomás looked closely at his friend. He didn't know how to ask the question, but he needed to know. "How's your dad?" he asked, not sure he wanted the truth. "Is he upset?"

Tommy felt the pressure of tears about to break loose, but he fought them back. He fiddled with a magazine someone had left behind on the library table and did not answer for a long time.

"I wouldn't exactly say he's upset," Tommy said. "I'd say he's more like furious, or crazed with anger. I wasn't sure if I was more scared he was going to hit me or that he was going to have a heart attack right there in our living room."

Tomás bit his lip. He knew Tommy's dad had a temper and that Mr. Martin had gotten more irritable in recent months as the family's business had fallen deeper into trouble.

"So I'm guessing I won't be coming over for dinner anytime soon," he joked.

"Might not be a good idea right now," Tommy said. "Maybe we should give it a little time. Ten or fifteen years might be good."

A look from the gray-haired woman at the front desk warned the boys to keep their voices down. They both knew Mrs. Davis, the librarian. She was always friendly away from the library. But, in here, her ears didn't miss a thing, and both boys knew she had a short fuse if she thought someone was being disruptive in the library.

Tommy scooted his chair closer to Tomás. He glanced at the computer screen in front of his friend. Pictures of baseball cards and baseball players covered it, like wallpaper.

"You find anything yet?" he whispered.

Tomás nodded, pointing at the screen as he spoke.

"It is pretty cool," he said. "I had no idea baseball cards had been around so long."

"What do you mean?" Tommy asked. "How long?"

"Says here the first baseball cards appeared sometime in the 1860s," Tomás said. "I didn't even know baseball was around back then, much less baseball cards. Some company named Peck & Snyder sold sporting goods and came up with the baseball cards to advertise its products."

Tommy looked back at the screen, reading about the history of baseball cards. When his eyes came to the section devoted to the 1952 Topps set, he scooted forward in his chair bringing his face closer to the screen.

"What do you see?" asked Tomás, who had been distracted by a sidebar about Peck and Snyder founders Andrew Peck and Irving Snyder.

"It says most everyone considers that 1952 set as the beginning of modern baseball cards," Tommy said. "The company took a black-and-white picture of each player, and then colorized it to use on the front of the cards. They added what they called a facsimile signature—like a picture of the player's actual autograph—for the first time ever. It says no one had ever done that before."

Tommy kept reading. "There were 407 cards in that set, and it was designed by a guy named Sy Berger. Another man, somebody named Woody Gelman, helped him, and they made the cards bigger than any cards in the past."

Tomás picked up reading from there. "It also says the 1952 cards were the first ones with a player's picture, the logo for the player's team, and the player's personal information and full career statistics on the back."

When he finished, Tomás noticed Tommy looking off into space. "Tommy?"

"Oh, sorry," Tommy said, shaking his head and refocusing on his friend. "I was just thinking. I don't understand why these particular cards are worth so much. Twenty thousand dollars for one pack of cards seems like an awful lot of money. That's more than a car costs! Is it just because they're so old?"

Tomás frowned. "I don't know. I've kind of wondered the same thing."

"I mean, there are other cards that are old, too, but lots of them are not worth much at all," Tommy said. "They print so many baseball cards—it's hard to imagine any of them ever being worth much."

"But they didn't print that many back in the early days," Tomás said. "This article says that's one of the reasons cards from that time are so valuable, because there weren't very many of them to start with compared to the millions of cards they print today."

"Okay, I guess that makes some sense," Tommy said, "but still one old printed bit of paper being worth more than my mother's car seems nuts to me."

His eyes returned to the article on the computer screen. "Hey, Tomás, did you ever buy a pack of cards with gum inside?"

"Not that I remember. Don't think I've ever seen one with gum inside. Why?"

"It says here that kids back in the 1950s bought a lot of the packs just for the big piece of gum that came inside," Tommy said. "And it says a lot of the time the kids just threw the baseball cards away because all they wanted was the gum anyway."

Tomás blew a long breath. "I bet they wish now they had thrown the gum away and kept some of those cards," he said, laughing until a cough by Mrs. Davis made him realize they were getting too loud again.

Tommy kept reading, scrolling down the page to see if he could find anymore about the 1952 Topps cards.

"Hey, it says here the 1952 Topps cards are the most famous cards in the history of baseball, and that the Mickey Mantle card in that set is the single most sought after card for collectors . . . but that set had a lot of famous players in it—people like Yogi Berra and Jackie Robinson."

"Jackie Robinson? Wasn't he the first African-American to play in the Major League Baseball?"

"That's right," Tommy said. "Man, that would have been scary. Can you imagine how they must have treated black players way back then, if people are still so racist today?"

Tomás squirmed in his chair. He knew all too well what it was like to be scared someone might hurt or hate you just because you were different. He looked at the long list of names on the screen and changed the subject. "It says there were a lot of Hall of Fame players in that 1952 set, but I've never heard of most of them. You ever heard of Duke Snider, Gil Hodges, Warren Spahn, Roy Campanella, or Eddie Mathews?"

"Don't think so," Tommy said. "I think I might have heard of the Snider guy, but not any of the others."

"It also mentions a player named Andy Pafko. Who's Andy Pafko?" Tomás asked. "I sure as heck have never heard of him."

"I don't know," Tommy said. "I've never heard of him either. But it says his card and the card for that Eddie Mathews guy are really hard to find in good condition."

"Says here kids used to keep their cards together with rubber bands," Tomás said, trailing his finger down the screen as he read. "Pafko's card was the first in the set and Mathews's card was number 407.

"Because most collectors back then kept their sets in numerical order, that put those two cards on the top and bottom of the stack and so they rubbed against the rubber band. It says the other cards were protected because they were on the inside, but those two cards almost always have rubber band marks or creases on them."

"I can see how that would happen . . . hey," Tommy said, something else catching his eye. "It says here almost all the cards back then were bought by kids, and one of the things they used to do was to clip the cards to the front axle of their bicycles—the cards supposedly made a cool sound when the spokes rubbed against the cards."

"That's crazy," Tomás said. "Why would they do that to their cards?"

"I guess because they had no idea those cards would be worth a lot of money sixty years later," Tommy said. "I mean we're twelve. Do we ever think about fifty or sixty years from now?"

"Not until this week," Tomás said, looking at Mrs. Davis and choking back a laugh. "I bet there are a lot of old men who wish they hadn't been quite so clever back then. Do you think the noise the cards made on their bikes was worth it?"

Tomás was too busy scrolling down the story to answer. He stopped suddenly. "Oh man. How sad is that?"

"What?"

"It says a lot of guys who bought baseball cards and collected them when they were kids went off to college or to the army and left all their cards at home in a closet or on a shelf in their old bedroom," he said.

"So," Tommy said. "What's sad about that? Couldn't they just go home and get them later?"

"Yeah, but by the time most guys realized their cards were worth something and went home to get them, the cards were gone. It says a lot of times their mom had thrown the cards away because she thought they were just taking up space," Tomás said.

"You're kidding! Why would their moms do that?" Tommy shouted outraged.

Tommy's outburst drew a disapproving look from Mrs. Davis. The boys gave a little wave of apology and scooted closer together, lowering their voices again.

"The moms thought the cards were old, which they were, and worthless, which they were not," Tomás read. "It says nobody really knows how many millions of dollars worth of baseball cards were thrown away by all those moms."

"That's almost funny," Tommy said. "It's sad if you're the guy who had collected them, but it's kind of funny, too."

Tommy kept reading only to burst out laughing again. Mrs. Davis came out of her chair this time, storming toward the boys as she removed her glasses.

"If you young men don't keep it down, I'm going to have to ask you to leave," she said in a loud whisper. "People here are trying to read."

Tommy looked around in all directions. He didn't see anyone but him and Tomás and he sure didn't see anybody reading. He kept that fact to himself. He didn't think pointing that out to Mrs. Davis would be such a great idea. He told himself her reaction was probably from force of habit; he knew how rowdy his classmates could get sometimes in the library after school.

"We're sorry, Mrs. Davis," Tomás said. "We'll be quiet."

Mrs. Davis stood over the boys another ten seconds, before giving them a little nod of warning and returning to her seat at the front desk.

"What were you laughing at?" Tomás asked.

"It gets worse," Tommy said with a smile.

"What could possibly be worse than your mother throwing away thousands of dollars of baseball cards?"

"Just listen to this," Tommy said. "It says the 1952 cards were printed in two series. The first series included cards one through 310, and came out in the spring and early summer. The second series included cards 311 through 407, and came out near the end of the season."

"Okay, so what?" Tomás said.

"The Mickey Mantle card was in that second series, and the company had trouble selling the cards that year, especially the second set because it came out so close to the end of the season," Tommy said.

"And?" said Tomás, growing a little impatient.

"It says the company had warehouses full of unsold cards in cases like the ones we found. Nobody knew who Mickey Mantle really was or would become, and they sure didn't know he was destined to be one of the best players in history, so the cards just didn't sell. That set wasn't worth anything, and the cards were just taking up space in the warehouse."

"Let me guess," Tomás said. "They burned them."

"Nope, they threw them in the ocean," Tommy said abruptly.

"You're kidding," Tomás said, his voice rising higher.

Tommy held his hands up to warn Tomás not to get too loud.

"No, I'm not kidding," Tommy whispered. "They rented a big boat a couple of years later and loaded up several thousand cases. They drove the boat out a few miles off the coast and dumped all those cards in the water."

"That's unbelievable," Tomás muttered.

"Can you imagine?" Tommy asked. "No telling how much those cards would be worth today."

Tomás exhaled long and slow, leaning back in his chair until he caught Mrs. Davis glaring at him again. Quietly, he lowered the chair back onto all four legs.

"All this just makes it harder for me to understand why your grandfather kept those cards hidden all that time and never told anyone," Tomás said. "I mean, you do think it was him who put them in the wall, don't you?"

"That's something I don't understand either," Tommy said. "I wish I could just ask him. It doesn't make sense that he would keep them in there even after the store was closed. It's been closed and empty for a long time, and a lot of things could have ruined those cards . . . rats, rain, vandals."

"Yeah, there were a lot of rats in that building," Tomás said shuddering at the memory. "I saw more evidence of them than I wanted to, and I can't believe none of them ever chewed on the boxes or anything."

"I know," Tommy said. "And there were three or four spots where the roof leaked, too. I can't believe no rain water ever reached them, or that the old building never burned down or anything. It's really a miracle that those cards are there at all, much less in perfect condition."

Tomás fell quiet, staring off into space.

"What's wrong?" Tommy asked.

"Oh, I was just wondering," Tomás answered.

Tommy's face broke into a wide smile. "I know what you're wondering," he said. "You're wondering how high the auction bids are up to, aren't you?"

Now it was Tomás's turn to smile. "Exactly. Let's get out of here and go by Mr. Coberly's office and find out."

Chapter 7

"Relax, Bill. This really is the best thing that could have happened. Think of it as a good thing."

Bill Martin looked wide-eyed at the man across the desk. He didn't look crazy, but Bill was still having serious doubts about his friend. "Good? This is good? How is this good? This could not possibly be good."

"Bill. You're yelling," the man said with a smile. "And, if you don't relax, you're going to have a stroke."

Bill Martin sat back, breathed in deeply and then slowly exhaled through his mouth. He rubbed his temples with the tips of his fingers, trying yet again to ease the headache that had plagued him since he saw Coberly's first press conference on television.

"Okay," Martin said, forcing himself to remain calm. "How is it a good thing that some Mexican kid is about to become a multimillionaire because he found a stash of rare baseball cards hidden inside a wall of my family's abandoned building? I don't see anything good about that."

Mark Wallis looked closely at his old friend and smiled. He'd known Bill Martin all his life. They'd both been born in San Moreno and had attended high school together, graduating in the Class of 1993.

"Bill, I'm your lawyer," Wallis said. "But I'm also your friend. I know the situation you're in. I know business isn't good. I know things are pretty tough on you right now."

Bill snorted. "Tough? No, Mark. It's much worse than tough. I'm six weeks from bankruptcy. I'm about to lose everything . . ."

Bill stopped in the middle of his sentence to take a long, deep breath, a desperate attempt to try and calm himself. Neither his son nor wife knew it, but just last week, the doctor had told him both his blood pressure and cholesterol were at dangerously high levels. His headaches had gone from frequent and painful to constant and nearly blinding in their intensity. The stress of a failing business was going to kill him, if his desperation over losing those silly baseball cards didn't do it first.

Mark picked up a pen and scratched a few notes on a yellow pad. "Bill, walk me through the conversation you had with this Martinez boy. I need to know exactly what was said."

"It wasn't really a big deal," Martin said. "I don't remember exactly because I wasn't really paying all that much attention."

Mark stopped writing, put his pen down slowly, and looked hard at his old friend. "Bill. This is a *really* big deal. This could be worth *tens of millions* of dollars." He put a strong emphasis on the amount. "So it's pretty important that you at least try to remember what you said."

Bill considered the advice. He wasn't a patient man by nature, but he realized Mark Wallis was right.

"I was in the truck and saw him on the sidewalk by the school," Martin began. "I pulled over and asked him if he could use fifty bucks. He said he could, so I handed him a key and told him to get all the junk out of that old Five & Dime store 'cause we were going to tear it down."

Mark held up a finger, motioning for Bill to stop.

"How old is this kid? Twelve?"

"Yeah," Martin said.

"Isn't that how old Tommy is?"

"Yeah, why?"

"I was just wondering why you didn't let Tommy clean it up and save yourself the fifty bucks if money is so tight, or at least let Tommy earn the money," Wallis said.

"Are you kidding me?" Martin said. "That place is a death trap with all that old junk in there and the roof half caved in. And then there are the rats that have taken over. I wouldn't let my kid in there alone for anything."

Mark Wallis looked at his friend closely again.

"But it's okay for this kid? Why? Because the kid is Hispanic?"

Mark Wallis knew Bill Martin wouldn't like being asked the question, but he might as well get used to it now.

"You know if we have to go to court, Sam Coberly's going to put you on the spot with that very question," he said.

"Yes, I know that," Martin said defensively. "And, no, it wasn't just because the Martinez kid is Mexican. You know me better than that, Mark."

Mark sat quietly, raising his eyebrows in response.

"Okay," Martin said finally. "Maybe I did think it was okay for the Mexican kid to go in there when I wouldn't let Tommy. So sue me. Does that make me a criminal? But I can tell you this, he was more than happy to go when he found out there was fifty bucks at stake. I was just helping him out. He was grateful."

"I'm sure he was," Wallis said, returning to his notes. "So what exactly was your agreement?"

"I already told you."

"No, I need to know exactly what you asked him to do and *exactly* what you told him about keeping anything he found in the building," Wallis said. "Word for word."

Bill Martin sat forward in his chair, putting his elbows on his knees and his head in his hands.

"That's part of my problem, Mark. I don't remember exactly what I said. I never really pay attention to my *exact* words. Who does?"

"I do," Wallis said. "And you should too, especially when it comes to business deals. Don't you see it matters in this case *exactly* what you said and *exactly* what your agreement was?"

Bill Martin let out a long, weary breath. "I told him to get it all out so I could knock the building down," Martin said. "And I said if he wanted any of the old junk he found in there he could keep it."

Again Wallis looked up at his old friend and client.

"Did you use the word 'junk' or some other word like that when referring to what he could keep?"

"I don't know exactly," Martin said. "But, if I didn't use that specific word, that's what I meant. He knew it and I knew it."

"Did he?"

"Did he what?"

"Did he know you meant he could only keep stuff you considered junk? Did you make that perfectly clear?"

"It was clear to me," Martin said angrily.

"But, don't you see, Bill? To legally prove that the boy had no claim to those cards, you have to be one hundred percent sure you made it clear he could not keep anything of value that he found," Wallis explained. "Otherwise, legally, the court could say you gave him permission to keep those cards."

Bill Martin stood angrily, fire in his eyes.

"But I didn't know they were there," Martin bellowed. "How could I have known those cards had been in that wall for sixty years? How could I tell the kid 'You can have anything you find in there except for the sixty million dollars worth of baseball cards hidden in the wall' when I didn't know the cards were even there?"

Wallis rose quickly, trying to regain control of the situation if only to keep his friend from having a heart attack in his office.

"Bill, I'm not saying you should have known," Wallis said calmly. "No one could have known. What I'm trying to get you to understand is that a judge can only decide ownership in this particular case based on what you said to Tomás Martinez. Your *exact* agreement is all that we have and really all that matters."

Bill threw himself back in his chair and covered his face with his hands.

"Mark, I honestly don't know what words I used," he said. "I know what I meant, but I really can't remember what exact words I used."

Wallis worded his next question very carefully.

"So what the boy says could be what happened? You could possibly have actually said Tomás Martinez could keep whatever he found there, so long as he removed it? No matter what you meant, is it possible that is what you said to him?"

"Yeah, it's possible," Martin said softly. "I just don't remember."

Wallis mulled that answer for a moment.

"Let me ask you this," Wallis finally said. "Could you tell a judge you don't think that's what you said—without being guilty of perjury? Would it be the truth if you testified that you don't think that's what you said?"

"But I already said it's possible I did say that," Martin protested.

"Forget about what's possible for a minute. Could you truthfully tell a judge you don't think that's what you said?"

44

Bill Martin's eyes lit up with a glimmer of hope. "Yeah, I could say that. I wouldn't be lying," Martin said smiling. "I don't think that's what I said. I really don't. It doesn't matter what's possible. All I have to do is keep telling them I don't think I said that."

He was up now, pacing the room. Wallis was writing furiously in his notepad.

"The kid can say whatever he wants," Martin said excitedly. "I say I don't think I said that, or just tell them I didn't say that, because in my mind that's not what I said."

"But, remember Bill," Wallis cautioned. "You can't tell a judge an outright lie, because that's perjury. You do that and you could go to jail on top of everything else."

"It's not lying," Martin said. "I don't remember saying he could keep whatever. What I remember, what I think—what I know in my heart—is that I told him he could keep whatever junk or trash he found."

"Was it 'junk' or was it 'trash' that you told him he could keep?" Wallis asked. "This is very important."

"What does it matter?"

"It has to be one specific word you can stick with," Wallis said. "I'm not telling you to perjure yourself. Don't lie, Bill. But you need to decide which specific word it was and stick with it."

Martin considered that carefully. "I'll say junk, because that sounds more like what I'd say to a little Mexican kid."

Mark raised his hand to get his friend's attention.

"Never, ever say anything like that out loud again while this case is going on," Wallis instructed. "You talk like that and there's not a judge in America that will find in your favor."

"Understood," Martin said. "So, now I say what I remember, and it's just my word against the Mexican kid's word. There's not a judge in Texas who's going to take the word of a little Mexican kid over the word of a respected white business owner."

The lawyer stopped writing, stood, and walked around his desk, so he could face his client without obstruction.

"I'm going to warn you again. Do not ever say anything like that outside this room, or you lose me as a lawyer and you automatically lose millions of dollars worth of rare vintage baseball cards. You have to watch what you say. People in this country today are sensitive to racially hateful talk—and those two things you just said are about as racially hateful as it gets. This kind of talk is beneath you Bill."

Now it was Bill Martin who held up his hand.

"Listen, Mark," he said. "You know the law and you know judges. But I know people, and I especially know the people from around here. Unless the judge is Mexican, there is no chance anybody is going to take the word of that twelve-year-old boy over a business owner and a leader in the community. And that's especially true when the boy happens to be Mexican. That's not hateful. That's just the way it is."

Wallis waited for him to finish, then spoke frankly.

"Haven't you forgotten one thing?" Wallis said. "What about the other person in this conversation?"

"What other person?" Martin asked. "Nobody else had a part in this so-called contract between me and the Martinez boy."

"No, but someone else did hear that conversation," Wallis said. "And that someone else supposedly heard you tell the boy he could keep anything he found."

Martin's face darkened and his voice lowered, becoming more serious.

"You're talking about Tommy."

"Of course I am," Wallis said. "I don't think it's going to help your case if you say one thing, the Martinez boy says another, and then your own son gets up and agrees with the kid."

Bill Martin pointed an angry finger at his old friend. "My boy is not and will not be part of this. He's confused about what was said, but that makes no difference to me. We will not drag him into this. We won't give him the chance to disagree with me about what was said."

Wallis stepped back behind his desk and picked up a stack of papers.

"You want me to file this restraining order to stop the auction for those cards, and to request a hearing to establish ownership, right?"

Bill Martin's eyes narrowed. "Of course," he said. "How else can we prove the cards rightfully belong to me and keep that lawyer from selling them out from under me?"

"If we file that motion and request a hearing for ownership, we won't have to drag your son into this, Bill," Wallis said. "Sam Coberly will do it for us."

"I hadn't thought of that," Martin admitted.

"So, what do we do?" Wallis asked. "Do we file these petitions with the court, knowing Sam's going to call your son as a witness against you? Or do we drop the legal fight and try to work out a compromise with the Martinez family over the cards?"

Bill Martin hesitated, but only for a moment.

"File the papers," he said firmly. "I don't want a compromise. I want it all."

Chapter 8

Tears filled Tomás's eyes as he hugged his father for the first time in six weeks. He held on tight, not wanting the embrace to ever end. Suddenly, the dam broke and tears rolled down his face. His father kissed the top of his head and assured him this ordeal would soon be over.

Despite what locals, like Bill Martin, might call him or his son, José Martinez was born an American citizen, just like them. His own mother—an illegal immigrant from Mexico—had given birth to him in an American hospital. José was thirteen when his parents were detained by immigration officers and eventually deported back to Mexico. He stayed in the United States, living with various relatives until he married Juana when he was eighteen.

Life for Juana and José had been good. They had a son. They both had jobs and their only child, Tomás, was in a good school. Last year, José had been promoted to yard boss at the local lumber company where he had worked for four years. And he and Juana had been saving money so they could purchase their first home.

A good man who loved his country and who had never been in trouble with the law, José went so far as to encourage his relatives back in Mexico who wanted to come to the U.S. not to come across the border illegally. He told them America was a country of great opportunity and promise, but only if people lived according to the laws and did what was right. It made him sad to see so many of his family members and other Mexican people begin their lives in America as lawbreakers, a designation they earned the moment they snuck across the US-Mexico border.

It was because of his outspoken determination to be a law-abiding citizen that José's arrest and conviction for embezzlement came as such a shock to the townspeople of San Moreno. It had been the previous fall when the lumber company's vice president noticed money missing from a weekend deposit. Because José had been the one who delivered the money to the bank, he became the first suspect.

Another employee then came forward to say he'd seen José removing money from the bag before leaving for the bank that day. José insisted he was innocent, but he also feared a jury might believe his coworker's story over his simply because the man was white.

With no money to hire an attorney of his own, José had a local lawyer appointed by the court to defend him. That attorney, whose own problems with Hispanics were

well known throughout the county, arranged a plea agreement that resulted in José's one-year prison sentence.

When the judge handed down his father's sentence,
Tomás had been devastated by the verdict, but he remained determined. Someday, he promised, he would
prove his father's innocence.

"Father, the money from these cards could be the answer," he said. "We can hire a lawyer—a real lawyer, like
Mr. Coberly, who knows what he's doing—who can prove
you did not take that money."

José cupped his son's cheek with his hand.

"By that time, my sentence will be over, and I will be
home," he said. "So what does it matter?"

Tomás looked up at his father, a man he admired above
anyone he had ever known.

"It matters because you are not a thief," Tomás said.
"If it takes the rest of my life, I will prove you did not take
that money because your honor and our family name are
at stake."

"And what are you doing to protect your own name?"
his father asked. "When the fight over these baseball cards
is finished, you have to make sure you can still walk the
streets with your head held high, knowing you did the
honorable and fair thing."

Tomás cast his glance down, unable to look at his father for a moment. "But, I've done nothing wrong."

"I know that, Tomás. I have never doubted that. You
have always made me proud." José said. "And there is nothing wrong with fighting for what is rightfully yours. But,

sometimes, when the fight is over, you realize that even though you were in the right, the fight was not worth what it cost for you to win. You might have been better off to compromise."

Not worth it? Compromise?

Tomás didn't understand.

"Father, they've told me this could be worth sixty million dollars for our family. How could any fight not be worth enough money to get you out of prison and prove your innocence, to make it where Mother no longer has to work such long hours at the hotel . . . to perhaps pay to bring some of our family to America legally . . . how could this fight not be worth that?"

"Those would all be wonderful things to spend the money from the baseball cards on, if it comes," his father agreed. "But none of them is worth having people doubting your honor, my son."

"How could anyone doubt my honor?" Tomás asked. "Mr. Martin told me I could keep anything I found in the old store that I wanted. I did not take anything that was not mine. I would never do that."

The guard started across the room toward them. Tomás and his father knew that meant their time was almost up.

"Son, whether it's six dollars or sixty million, it's not worth having if people see you in the wrong," his father said softly. "I know you're not in the wrong in this case, and you know you're not in the wrong. But, if everyone else believes you have *done* wrong, that may be all that matters in the end."

"I understand, Father," Tomás said, quietly. "So what should I do?"

"Stand up for yourself," his father answered quickly. "I'm not saying to give up the cards without a fight. I'm saying to remember that winning and getting the money is not more important than keeping your good name—no matter how much money is involved."

*****

Sam Coberly put the key in the lock, turned the handle on his front door, and stepped into the air-conditioned comfort of his two-story house. He had lived in south Texas his entire life, but he had never gotten used to the humid summer heat. He was one of those people who kept his air conditioner set so low that his windows frosted over in August.

He tossed his keys into a small dish on the table near the foyer and reached down to scoop up the mail the letter carrier had dropped through the slot on the door.

It had been a good day. Long, but good. He'd been on the telephone most of the afternoon, doing interviews about the baseball card lawsuit with reporters from Orlando to San Francisco.

He had even spoken with one newspaper reporter from London, fitting since the precursors to baseball cards were Trade Cards, a mix of art and advertising created by London businesses to woo customers back in the seventeenth century.

He flipped through the mail as he strolled into the kitchen. On the counter, the message light blinked on the telephone. He pushed the play button and listened in stunned silence as a muffled voice played back.

"Mr. Coberly, I hope you had a good day," the voice said. "I know it was a busy day, since I watched you leave your house for work just after 7:30 this morning. You stopped at the coffee shop on the way to your office, arriving at work at exactly eight o'clock. You did the very same thing yesterday. Did you know that?

"You didn't leave the office again until lunch, when you walked down to the café for the rotary club meeting. You sat next to Bill Wofford, the bank president, and had the pot roast and two rolls. You really are going to have to start eating better, Sam.

"You walked back to work and spent the entire afternoon in your office, mostly on the phone. I know that because I could see you through your office window.

"And now, Mr. Coberly, you've just come home and picked up your mail, but, what you don't know, Sam, is that you received something extra today—sort of a special delivery. But it's not in your mail. It's in your bedroom, on the pillow of your bed. Don't worry it isn't a bomb or anything," the man on the recording said and chuckled softly. "It's just a little note to let you know we were there.

"By the way, you have a very nice home, Mr. Coberly. We would hate for something to happen to it. If memory serves, it's been in your family for more than a hundred years, hasn't it? I would, however, suggest you get rid of the shag carpet in the den—a little dated don't you think, but that's just my opinion.

"Anyway, I wanted to let you know that the community of San Moreno is behind you in this baseball card disagreement and that you have a lot of people watching your every move. Don't forget that. Have a wonderful evening, Mr. Coberly."

Sam reached out with a shaking hand and tapped the stop button. A cold sweat had broken out on his forehead as he turned and headed into the bedroom.

Chapter 9

Juana Martinez shook with anger as she surveyed the living room. Her home was trashed. While they had been at the prison visiting José, someone had broken into their home, ransacked the entire house, and stolen their television and two stacks of DVD movies.

Both front windows were broken, and the front door had been kicked in with such force that it hung by just its bottom hinge. The glass from the broken windows covered the front porch, meaning they had been broken from the inside. Furniture was overturned, light fixtures had been ripped out of the ceiling, and the couch cushions were shredded and scattered across the living room floor.

This was not the work of a burglar out to steal a television. This was mean, vindictive vandalism. The person who had done this had done it out of anger or hatred, or maybe to intimidate. But the broken windows and destroyed furniture weren't the worst of it. The intruders had used red and black spray paint to scrawl in huge letters on the living room wall where the television set had been: "THIEVES" and "GO BACK TO MEXICO." She could not bear to repeat the profanity sprayed on the wall over her sofa.

A noise behind gave her a start.

"Anything taken?"

It was an officer responding to her 9-1-1 call. She turned to see an enormous man opening the screen door and stepping into the living room. He was followed by a second, smaller officer, a man who seemed hesitant to enter the house.

"I'm Officer Hodges," the taller man said. "This is Officer Wilkins. Someone reported a break-in at this address."

"That was me," Juana said.

Even though they were police officers, she was a little uncomfortable with the two men being in her house without her husband present, but she told herself the officers were there to help.

"They broke down our door, stole our television and about twenty DVDs, and wrote horrible things on our walls," Juana said.

The taller officer glanced back at his partner and then turned his attention to Juana again. "Anything taken that actually belonged to you?" he asked with a smirk.

The question caught Juana off guard, but then she understood. He was assuming that she or someone in her family had stolen the television in the first place and that it did not actually belong to them. She didn't respond to his question because she wasn't sure how to respond.

After a moment of silence, the smaller officer joined the conversation.

"Could be someone from this neighborhood," he said flatly. "These people are always stealing, even from each other."

Looking around her ransacked living room, Juana turned back to the officers in disbelief.

"So are you trying to say this had nothing to do with this whole baseball card thing?" she asked.

"I don't know. I guess it's possible," Officer Hodges said with a wink that Juana found insulting. "Can't say I blame them. I guess they think if your husband steals from them, and your son steals from them, then they've got a right to steal from you."

Juana was shocked at the officer's attitude, but somehow held her temper in check. These men were law enforcement officers. They deserved respect. Fighting with the local police could never help her family, and that was her first concern. She took a deep breath before responding.

"Officer, my husband did not steal, and my son did not steal," she said firmly. "But that has nothing to do with my home being vandalized. Whoever did this had no right to do so . . ." She stopped, fighting back tears.

"It's not like it's really your home," the smaller officer said rudely. "Actually belongs to Mr. Sandifer, doesn't it? You're just renting like everyone else in this part of town."

A voice came from the porch as the screen door opened. "Did you get all that, Mike? I think that should play well on tonight's broadcast."

Sam Coberly stepped through the door, followed by an African-American man in khaki slacks and a pink polo shirt. Behind them, a third man held a television camera.

"What's going on here, Mr. Coberly?" the taller officer said in an angry voice. "We don't need any television cameras here. This is a simple case of breaking and entering."

Coberly glanced at Juana, smiling to reassure her.

"Oh, I believe there is a great need for television cameras wherever you two young gentlemen go," Coberly said firmly. "Especially in this neighborhood where you've had so many problems in the past with the locals."

The man in the pink shirt stepped forward, offering his hand. "Brian Singleton, KVST television, San Antonio." He looked at the taller officer's badge closely. "You would be officer . . . ?"

"Robert Hodges," Coberly said, by way of introduction. "And that would be Patrolman Randall Wilkins over there," he said, pointing to the shorter officer.

Officer Hodges was not impressed. "What are you doing here, Coberly? And why are they here?"

Sam Coberly stepped past the officer and took out a cigar. He didn't light it, but began chewing on the end as he spoke.

"Mrs. Martinez actually phoned me before she called the police," Coberly said. "And, since I keep a police scanner going at all times in my office and in my car, I heard the names of the two officers who would be responding—that being the two of you. Because of your difficulties in the past in this neighborhood, I felt it might be wise if we had a witness. Mr. Singleton was headed here anyway to do an interview with the Martinezes about the baseball cards, so I would say it all worked out nicely."

Sam couldn't help smiling with great satisfaction that his hunch had proved correct.

Officer Hodges stepped closer to the lawyer, attempting to intimidate the much older man. Coberly simply smiled and chewed his cigar. He knew the law and he knew their rights.

"How long have they been here and how long has that camera been running?" Hodges asked threateningly.

"Long enough," Coberly said. "In fact, I believe that camera may still be on."

Coberly looked around the officer toward Singleton.

"Brian, would you check for us please? I believe your associate forgot to turn off his camera, and it may still be recording. We wouldn't want the battery to run down."

The reporter glanced at Mike the cameraman, who gave him the "thumbs up" sign and stepped out onto the porch. Officer Hodges started for the door, but stopped short when the TV reporter stepped into his path.

"Officer Hodges, can you explain your disrespectful attitude with Mrs. Martinez? Surely it is not because she is Hispanic, because that would be a violation of her civil rights, an insult to the badge you wear, and a crime against the law you are sworn to uphold," Singleton said.

Hodges glared at the reporter, who was a good two inches taller than him but not nearly as thick through the middle.

"You're not authorized to be here," Officer Hodges said. "And I'll be needing that videotape because you don't have permission to be here. If you broadcast so much as a second of that, you'll end up in jail, and I'll sue your station from here to New York."

Sam gave a quick cough to get Hodges's attention. The officer begrudgingly turned to look at the lawyer.

"What is it, Coberly?"

"These two men have every right to be here," Sam Coberly said, grinning broadly. "If you recall, they were invited here by Mrs. Martinez to do a story on the baseball cards. They were simply in the process of shooting background video on the front porch when they happened to record your conversation with Juana through that broken window."

Officer Hodges stepped back, frowning at Coberly. Oh how he hated lawyers, especially this local one.

"Well, isn't that an amazing coincidence," he said.

"I'll grant you that," Coberly answered. "Now, if you two officers are finished with your so-called investigation, I'm sure you'd like to return to your station to speak with your captain before Mr. Singleton calls him for a comment on this video footage."

For the first time since Coberly had arrived, Officer Wilkins seemed interested in the conversation. "You can't do that," he protested. "That'll cost us our jobs."

"I'm afraid it could end up costing you quite a bit more than just your badge, Officer Wilkins," Coberly said. "In light of your past problems with people in this neighborhood, and what's on that videotape, I'm afraid you may find yourself before a judge."

Coberly paused for effect while Wilkins squirmed.

"You might even go to jail," Sam said. "Now wouldn't that be ironic?"

He paused, letting the idea sink in.

"Then again, you should have thought about that before you insulted and intimidated my client and ran all over her civil rights," Coberly said. "Have a nice day, officers."

Officer Hodge's face was now bright pink and veins twitched near his temple. He clenched and unclenched his fists several times before quietly walking out the door with Wilkins following along after him.

Singleton smiled as the door slammed behind the two men.

"Nice guys," he said. "Makes you sleep better at night knowing men like that are out there protecting you from the bad people of the world."

Coberly stepped over a broken lamp and sat slowly on the torn brown leather couch.

"Thankfully, most police officers are not like these two, but there are a few bad apples, and our community is the worse for it," he said. "But the local police chief, Merle Henderson, is a good man. I think he does his best to treat everyone fairly—even knuckleheads like Hodges and

Wilkins. He gave them a chance to change their ways. Now he'll have their badges before tomorrow morning, and he'll make sure they never wear one again."

Singleton slipped his reporter's notebook in his pants pocket and reached out to shake Coberly's hand.

"I owe you, Sam. Big time," he said. "This story has everything, including common interest out the wazoo—and stories like this don't come around often. I can guarantee this will go national."

"Ridiculous," Coberly said. "I've been in court a dozen times in five years trying to get those two boys off the force, I just never had the evidence to make it stick. You've done Juana, the whole county, and me a huge favor. You owe me nothing."

For the first time since Coberly and the reporter had arrived, Juana spoke.

"I want to thank both of you so much," she said. "Will this be on the television news?"

"Are you kidding?" Singleton said. "Like I was telling Mr. Coberly, this will most likely be on every TV station in the country. With all the attention that's already on this whole baseball card find, and then to have these two officers so blatantly confront you given their record with the Hispanic community? My editor might even break into programming and push this on as a Special Report."

The TV reporter walked over to Juana and extended his hand; it covered Juana's tiny one like a catcher's mitt. "You are a brave and amazing woman," he said. "By the time this day is over, people from coast to coast will have seen how local law enforcement let you down in your time of need, and most people will recognize them for the ignorant bigots they are."

Juana nodded a wordless thank-you to the reporter, then turned to Coberly.

"Does that man, Patrolman Wilkins, have any relatives who live around here?"

"He has two brothers, I believe," Coberly said. "Why?"

"His last name is the same as the man who was the main witness against my husband," she said. "Because of the lies that man told, my husband is in prison for something he did not do."

Her words brought Coberly to his feet again, chewing hard on what was left of his cigar.

"Well, that's quite interesting," Coberly said. "Don't you think that's interesting, Mr. Singleton?"

Brian Singleton didn't answer. He was too busy writing in his notebook.

Chapter 10

Tomás backed up against the lockers, his books held in front of him for protection.

"What do you want, Hudson?"

Hudson Mitchell was three months older and six inches taller than Tomás. He also weighed about fifty more pounds. He had a reputation as a bully, but he had never given Tomás any problems before. Partly that was because Tomás did all he could to avoid people like Hudson Mitchell—in and out of school. Partly it was because Hudson was usually serving some kind of suspension at school, so he wasn't normally free to roam the halls with other students.

Hudson jabbed a finger at Tomás, striking his textbooks hard. "You're not too popular these days, wetback," he said. "Can't believe you walk around by yourself. Aren't you afraid some law-abiding person might decide to teach you a lesson? I want those baseball cards. They should belong to a real American."

Before Hudson had started talking, Tomás had been terrified. He was no fighter, and he had no doubt Hudson Mitchell could beat him up without breaking a sweat. But the words coming out of the bully's mouth infuriated him.

"So what are you going to do, Hudson, beat me up?" Tomás asked with more courage than he felt. "If you do, you get kicked out of school again for, what, the fourth time this semester? Don't you ever get tired of getting kicked out of school?"

Caught off guard (his victims rarely dared challenge him) Hudson stepped back, looking at Tomás as if he had gone insane. Tomás used the hesitation to his advantage.

"Beat me up, if you must—but it won't get you the baseball cards and it will, I can promise, get you suspended again," Tomás said with a weak attempt at a laugh. "And another thing . . . I'm not a wetback, as you say. I'm an American citizen, and as real an American as you. I was born here and I've lived in San Moreno all my life."

His bluff almost worked, but then Hudson must have remembered his size and weight advantage, because he hit Tomás in the side of the head with a blow that felt like a sledgehammer striking a melon. When Tomás hit the floor, his head was spinning; Hudson Mitchell was standing over him.

"No," Hudson said calmly. "It doesn't bother me at all to get kicked out of school again."

Three minutes later, Tomás received a detention for being late to history class. Hudson Mitchell was never called to the office, even after the principal was told about the altercation in the hall.

So much for the perks of being famous, Tomás thought.

*****

It had not been exactly a great day for Sam Coberly, either. He had gotten another phone call. This time, at the office. The voice on the phone was again muffled, as if someone had covered the receiver with a cloth and was speaking through it. The message wasn't quite as friendly as the last time, so Sam decided to call the police after the caller hung up.

Eight minutes later, police cars and fire trucks surrounded Sam Coberly's downtown law offices, and a huge crowd had gathered behind the caution tape at the next intersection down. The police chief found Coberly there and pulled him aside.

"Any idea who it was?" Chief Merle Henderson asked, looking hard at Sam Coberly.

"Nothing I could prove, but I have some suspicions," Sam said. "Let me guess. The call came from the pay phone down by the old grocery store?"

Chief Henderson looked at Coberly suspiciously. "How did you know that?"

"Because even though this caller was obviously crazy to pull a stunt like this, he's most likely not stupid. He knows that phone calls can be traced with today's technology, and that you would easily locate the phone he called from. Not many people know that old pay phone still works, and he knew it couldn't be traced back to him."

The police chief nodded at the lawyer's reasoning. Chief Henderson gestured toward Coberly's building, a safe distance down the street from them.

"Are the cards still locked in your office?"

Coberly looked shocked, even slightly insulted. "Chief Henderson, do I look that stupid?"

The police chief smiled.

"I'll take the fifth on that Sam. Either way, I'm not going to ask you exactly where they are. I'm not sure I want to know," he said. "But I am hoping they are somewhere safe."

"Very safe," the attorney said. Coberly looked past the police chief toward his office building. "You know there most likely are no bombs in there?"

Chief Henderson grunted, then removed a notepad from his shirt pocket, opened it, and started making notes.

"So exactly what did this person say, Sam?"

"Well, the conversation was very short and one-sided," Coberly said. "I don't have a secretary, so I answered the phone. All he said was that the building was going to blow up."

Chief Henderson looked up, waiting for more.

"And then?"

"Then he hung up," Coberly said. "I started to ignore the call and go on about my business, but I realized there might just be a few people in this town stupid enough to actually put a bomb of some kind in my office. So I gave you boys a call."

"Well, that was a smart decision on your part," Chief Henderson said. "But you do realize it doesn't have to have been someone from San Moreno? I mean this story has made international headlines; it could have been anyone on the planet."

Coberly was shaking his head.

"I don't think so, Merle," he said. "When I answered, they didn't ask if I was Sam Coberly, and they didn't ask to speak to Mr. Coberly. The caller just said, 'Is that you, Sam?' That tells me it was someone who knows me."

The chief scratched a few more notes, and then turned to address a uniformed officer approaching from the direction of Coberly's law office. "Well, officer?"

"Nothing Chief," the bomb squad member said.

"You sure?"

"We've been over that entire building four times, top to bottom," the officer said. "There's nothing there, and never has been, or our dogs would have alerted on it."

As the officer spoke, a flash of light and an eruption like a thunderclap shook the street, rattling windows for a half-mile in every direction. Sam Coberly's 1979 Pontiac Bonneville burst into flames as the explosion lifted the car off the pavement in front of the law office. The car, now missing its doors, came to rest sideways in the street.

The police chief blinked, scowled, and started barking orders at his men, telling them to move the crowd back.

Coberly stood dumbstruck, his eyes glued to the burning mass of his beloved Bonneville.

"Well that's inconvenient," Coberly said, letting out a huge sigh.

Chief Henderson removed his hat and wiped the sweat off his forehead with the back of his right hand.

"Could have been worse," he said. "You could have been in it when it blew up."

Sam Coberly smiled weakly, reaching for his cell phone in his inside jacket pocket.

"That's true," Coberly said. "That would have been bad, for me at least."

He tried to muster a laugh, but just couldn't, as he watched flames devour what was left of his old car.

"You know, Merle, it's not just that some idiot blew up my car," the attorney said. "What really irks me is that I had new brakes and new tires put on her this month. Cost me twelve hundred dollars."

Chief Henderson glanced over at the burning wreckage of Coberly's Pontiac.

"Would it hurt your feelings if I told you I never did like that car?"

Chapter 11

"Why don't you people get a life?"

Bill Martin had always wondered why celebrities complained about reporters and photographers. Now he was beginning to understand.

It had been less than a week since the story about the baseball cards had first made news. To Martin, it seemed like it had been going on for months. Day and night, television news crews parked outside his house, their vans and trucks lining the street on both sides. Camera flashes erupted every time he or his wife opened the front door or drove out of the driveway.

Two times he thought he had managed to sneak away without their knowledge. But later that evening—on both occasions—he had ended up seeing television news footage of himself, apparently shot by a photographer he had never even known was around. Reports of his legal efforts—his very legal, legal efforts, he might note—to stop the sale of the baseball cards had hit the media firestorm and caused another explosion of coverage. It was like throwing gasoline on a small flame. It was now a bonfire.

Specifically, his lawsuit asked the judge to put a temporary hold on the selling of the cards, meaning they could not legally be sold until the court had determined who the rightful owner was. It seemed a reasonable request to Martin.

You would never, however, gather that from the television coverage. The focus of the news stories had shifted over the last few days. The first reports during the initial media frenzy had been about the amazing discovery—everyone loves a buried treasure story. But then the media's attention had moved to the struggling Martinez family and its twelve-year-old hero.

That story, Martin knew, made for great human interest—catnip for newspaper editors and TV news directors.

The latest twist to the story in the past twenty-four hours centered on the custody dispute and exactly what agreement had been struck between Bill Martin and Tomás Martinez.

Rumors of Bill Martin's financial struggles had begun circulating, and he knew it was only a matter of time until the whole world knew his company was about to go under. To make matters worse, at this point in the story, most of the world had pegged Bill Martin for the bad guy. Having heard multiple radio segments, read numerous national newspaper articles, and seen hours of TV reports about it, Bill Martin had come to realize that no matter who told the story, it made him look like Ebenezer Scrooge, a mean, nasty, money-grubbing old miser who was suing a twelve-year-old (a twelve-year-old who just wanted to help his destitute family) over some baseball cards.

Had he been anyone else watching the reports on television, Bill Martin had to admit he would have hated him, too.

Meanwhile, the coming court fight over the ownership of the cards had done nothing to slow the number of bids pouring into the auction. He hadn't checked today, but the last bid he had heard was somewhere in the neighborhood of thirty million dollars. He laughed because otherwise he would have had to cry.

Thirty million dollars for six boxes of baseball cards . . .

Bill Martin still could not believe it. It was like a dream—or a nightmare, depending on what character you were in the story. The whole thing didn't seem real. But the irony of the situation didn't escape him. For years, he had spent most of his waking hours playing in and then eventually working at the old Five & Dime alongside his father. He thought back to the countless summer days spent checking people out at that very counter while all the while the cases of baseball cards were hidden behind a thin wall of paneling just a few feet away.

What had father been thinking? Worse yet, through all the years of his childhood, Bill Martin could not remember his father once bringing him home, or giving him, a pack of baseball cards, even though the old man knew how much Bill loved the game. *Maybe he only saw the cards as a commodity*, Bill thought.

If that was the case, the old man had been proven right. And it wasn't like Bill Martin wanted to kill the worldwide interest in the cards. On the contrary, he wanted the bids to go as high as possible. He just wanted things slowed down so that when the final ridiculous bid was made and the cards finally sold, he would be the one cashing the enormous check.

When he had told Wallis to file suit, he'd been a little afraid the restraining order might scare off potential bidders. But the explosion of coverage set off by his legal moves had ended up having the complete opposite effect. It had taken less than twenty-four hours for the bid to reach the thirty-million-dollar plateau. The very thought of that much money made him dizzy.

The week was now behind them, and maybe the weekend would bring some much needed quiet. It being Friday night, his wife and son were at church for some kind of prayer meeting. Bill was somewhere he hated with a passion: the parking lot of the local Walmart Supercenter. He had gone to pick up something for his headaches, and because he had run out of frozen tamale dinners. He hadn't seen any cameras on his way into the store, so he thought maybe the reporters had taken off for the night.

He could not have been more wrong. The baseball cards had become a 24/7 story. When he left the store, he saw four of them, all doing that backward walking thing in front of him so they could take footage of Bill walking to his truck. *How pathetic is that?* He could already hear the network anchor that night, describing the video as viewers sat mesmerized on their couches all over America.

"And here's Bill Martin as he heads back to his beat-up pickup truck after buying aspirin and a frozen dinner. No one knows for sure what might happen next."

That's when he stopped, hand on his front door, and screamed at the photographers to "Get a life." His outburst must have shocked them, because for a second all four looked a little confused. He took the opportunity to jerk open the door, slide in, and start the truck—all in one motion.

The national news crew recovered first and moved to film him driving away. Bill really should have ignored them and instead checked his rearview mirror before backing out of the parking space, but the lights on the cameras had him flustered.

The crunch of metal against metal was sickening, even if he wasn't going all that fast. He knew without looking what had happened. The only question was whom he had hit and how bad the damage would be.

He would never have dreamed a little fender-bender in a parking lot could have international news interest until he glanced over his shoulder and saw Juana and Tomás Martinez getting out of a 1998 Ford Taurus that now had significant damage to the right front fender.

Chapter 12

Tomás had a bad feeling about the game. Not a bad feeling that his team, the Astros, was going to lose. He had a lot of confidence in his team, even against the Dodgers. No this feeling had more to do with the unusually large crowd of people who had showed up for his Saturday afternoon twelve-and-under baseball game.

Tomás and his Astros team were the champions of the San Moreno Hispanic League, and they were playing the Dodgers, the champions of the San Moreno City League. Nobody could tell you why the town's Junior League baseball teams were still divided into what everyone called the "White League" and the "Mexican League." But they were.

Every year for the past four seasons, the Astros had won the Mexican League title and the Dodgers had come in first in the White League.

The first three years, the Dodgers had also beaten the Astros in the county championship game. Then last year, Tomás's first year playing shortstop for the Astros, his team had beaten the Dodgers 6-1 for its first ever County League Championship.

This year was Tommy's first season to play for the Dodgers, and he had turned out to be the team's best player, a double-threat pitcher/hitter. So far this season when Tommy pitched, the Dodgers won. When Tommy wasn't pitching, he played second base, and he had already hit four home runs, three triples, and eight doubles.

The Dodger coaches had handpicked all the best white players in town, while the coaches for the Astros had done the same thing in the Hispanic neighborhoods. The result was two very good teams—neither of whose fans would be happy with a loss in the championship game.

That was especially true this year. If Dodger fans had wanted to beat the Astros in years past, they hoped to embarrass the team this year. If Astros fans had been happy when they had knocked off the Dodgers last year, they would be overjoyed to beat the all-white team this particular summer.

And it was all because of the baseball card war.

As luck would have it, the Dodgers were hoping this year to win the title for a brand new sponsor: Bill Martin Construction. The Astros, on the other hand, had been sponsored for the fifth year in a row by Samuel Coberly, Attorney at Law. The pairing could not have been more perfectly poetic, or more explosive.

So far this summer, the two teams had played twice already, with each team winning once. In the first game, Tommy had pitched for the Dodgers and had struck out eleven Astros batters. Tomás was happy for his best friend, especially since he had managed to get three hits off Tommy and scored his team's only run in a 4-1 loss.

In the second game, just two weeks ago, the Astros pitcher had walked Tommy all four times he was at bat. Tomás had three more hits and drove in the winning run. The Astros won 3-2.

Every time the two teams had played for the county championship, there had been a packed house—half white and cheering for the Dodgers, half Hispanic and rooting for the Astros. Both crowds, mostly parents and relatives of the boys on the field, were loud and passionate in their support for their team. But this year there was a little extra interest in the county championship game.

Tomás tied his cleats, grabbed his glove, and walked out of the dugout onto the field to start warming up. The Dodgers were already on the field in their white uniforms with blue script, just like the Major League Dodgers from Los Angeles wore. The Astros were wearing their gray pants and red shirts.

Tomás glanced toward the bleachers and dropped the baseball he had been about to toss to Hernando Motta, the Astros catcher. There had to be more than five hundred people crammed onto two sets of metal bleachers behind first and third base. Unbeknownst to Tomás, both sets of bleachers had filled to capacity more than an hour before the game was scheduled to start. Mobs of latecomers—the smart ones had brought lawn chairs—were forced to find a vacant spot where ever they could outside the fence.

Tomás looked down the right field line, across the outfield toward left field, and then back down the fence line toward home plate.

He guessed another five hundred people circled the field, and more people were still crowding into the park. And then there were the cameras. Tomás counted at least eleven television cameras set up at various places around the field. It was like the World Series what with all the crowd and all the TV cameras.

"Can you believe this?"

Tomás turned and saw his best friend walking up. Tommy and Tomás had been inseparable for sometime. Everyone knew it. But Tomás also knew his teammates wouldn't be too happy about them chatting just before they "went to war" against each other.

"It's ridiculous," Tomás said. "There must be a thousand people and almost a dozen TV cameras here."

"I just overheard somebody say there were close to a fifteen hundred people in the stands and ballpark," Tommy said. "But you're right about the cameras. There are a dozen of them, all broadcasting live. I think they're actually going to broadcast the whole game. Can you believe that? Our twelve-and-under county championship broadcast live?"

"I noticed something else," Tomás said. "Did you see there's one white umpire and one Mexican umpire. Don't think I remember that from previous years. Wonder if it is on purpose."

"You know it is," Tommy said. "I guess they wanted to do whatever they could to make sure nobody could blame the umpires if they lost."

Tomás heard a voice booming from across the field near the Dodger dugout.

"Hey, Martin! You gonna play with us, or are you Mexican now?"

Neither Tommy nor Tomás had to turn to see who had hollered. They both recognized that voice. It was Hudson Mitchell, first baseman for the Dodgers and the guy who had already tried to start a fight with Tomás at school about the baseball cards.

"Be right there," Tommy shouted back. He turned to Tomás, smiled, and stuck out his hand. "Gotta run. Have a good game and watch out. Hudson is pitching today, and I'd bet money that he's gonna throw at least one pitch right at your head."

Tomás reached out and shook Tommy's hand.

"Good luck to you, too," Tomás said. "And don't worry about me. Hernando told me everyone on the team is just waiting for a chance to charge the mound tonight, preferably with Hudson on it. Apparently I'm not the first guy on this team he's tried to pick a fight with."

While the coaches for each team approached home plate for pregame instructions from the umpires, Tomás headed back to the dugout. He glanced again through the fence at the mass of people who had come out to watch the game. It was a little too easy to see the fans were divided by race. Most of the people on the first base bleachers and standing along the right field fence were Hispanic and yelling for the Astros. On the other side, packed onto the third base bleachers and all down the left field fence were hundreds of Dodgers fans, most of them white.

Tomás felt a shiver run down his back. *Hope Hudson is the only trouble brewing tonight*, he thought.

That's when he realized someone else, besides Tommy and him, had anticipated trouble at the game: a dozen or so sheriff's deputies and police officers stood outside the fence behind home plate. Twelve lawmen to control more than a thousand people didn't seem like good odds, but Tomás hoped he was wrong.

The first pitch had yet to be thrown, but several minor disagreements had already arisen. Tomás saw two women, one white and one Hispanic, screaming at each other in the stands, probably over seating. In front of the concession stand, two men had to be pulled apart after they got into a shoving match over who was next in line.

Tomás grabbed a paper cup and filled it with cold water from the thermos near the dugout entrance. At home plate, his coach, Mauricio Motta, was speaking loudly to the Dodger coach, Hudson Mitchell's father, Kendall.

Something appeared to be wrong.

Kendall Mitchell stepped into Mauricio, jabbing his finger into the Astros coach's chest. Mauricio knocked the man's hand away and stepped back, and Tomás saw the white umpire step between the coaches. Tomás was about to breathe a sigh of relief when something happened that he would never forget. The same umpire, a man named Jason Jackson, managed to push Kendall Mitchell back toward his dugout. But then, as fast as lightning, he spun back to Mauricio Motta and struck him across the face with his fist, knocking the Astros coach to the ground.

The crowd was on its feet in an instant, roaring as the Astros coach struggled to get up. A moment later, Jackson was struck from behind, tackled by his peer, the other umpire. The two umpires rolled around home plate, kicking, punching, and scratching one another. Taking their cue from the two men charged with enforcing sportsmanship and decorum on the diamond, the crowd of more than one thousand people poured onto the field.

The adults had spoken.

What they didn't notice was that players on both teams had managed to sneak out of the dugouts and away from the action as a dozen television cameras carried the entire brawl live to two hundred million viewers around the world.

Had the cameras bothered to scan the bleachers, they would have found them empty save for two figures sitting in the very top row of the first base stand. One was the mother of the most famous player on the Astros team. The other was an old man with a disgusted look on his face, chomping on a cigar.

Chapter 13

Bill Martin removed the gas nozzle from his truck, placed it back on the pump, and screwed the lid to his gas tank back on. Just as he was about to open the door and slide into the truck, he heard someone call his name from the door of the station.

As he was trying to figure out who had hollered at him, Randall Wilkins stuck his head between the two pumps, a beer in one hand.

"Hey, Bill. You got a minute?"

Bill Martin did not care much for Randall Wilkins or any of his family. All were hard to get along with and all had been bullies as far back as Martin could remember.

"What do you need, Randy?"

"Just want to talk with you for a minute," Wilkins whined.

Martin closed the truck door and stepped around the pumps to where Wilkins stood next to his black Ford F150 four-wheel drive pickup, the bottle of beer still in his right hand. One of his brothers—Bill couldn't remember his name—sat in the passenger seat, also holding a beer.

"Should you be driving with an open container, Randy?" Martin said. "Drinking and driving are still against the law, and you being a police officer and all . . ."

Wilkins took a long pull on the beer, threw the bottle in a trash can near the gas pumps, and spit on the ground not far from Martin's foot.

"Not anymore," he said.

"It's not against the law anymore?" Martin asked, not understanding.

"No, I'm not a cop anymore," Wilkins said angrily. "Got fired 'cause of that sleazy Mexican woman and that black news reporter."

Inside the truck, the other Wilkins brother laughed out loud, drawing a stern look from the former police officer. Bill still couldn't remember the brother's name, but he did remember him working at a lumberyard in town a couple of years back.

"Look, Randy," Martin said. "I'm really busy and I'm not having a great day. What do you need?"

Wilkins pulled a round can out of his front pocket and put a huge wad of snuff inside his bottom lip. He spit twice on the ground before he continued.

"I don't need anything, Bill," he said. "I just came to tell you we got your back, me and some of the boys."

"Got my back? How? Why?"

"Over this deal with the Mexican kid who stole your baseball cards," Wilkins said, as if any idiot should have known what he was talking about. "Even if you lose in court, those people ain't gonna end up with those cards or the sixty million dollars, or whatever it ends up being."

Now Bill Martin was more than a little uncomfortable. He might not like Mexicans, but he didn't consider himself a racist like Randall Wilkins. For years he'd heard rumors about a secret group operating around San Moreno, something akin to the Ku Klux Klan. Nobody talked about it out loud, but there were whispers. The group was supposedly a violent band of "true believers" known to have been behind many a hate crime in the community.

"And how would you and your boys take care of it?" Martin asked, not sure he wanted to know the answer.

Wilkins flashed a wicked grin. "Encouragement. We see wetbacks like that boy and his mama causing trouble, and we encourage them to remember who they are."

"So you're the ones who trashed their house?" Martin asked. He had read about the home invasion in the local newspaper.

"Not me, no sir," Wilkins said innocently. "At the time of that particular break-in, I was an upstanding law enforcement officer. But, if they had asked me who done it, I might could have told them."

Bill Martin knew he should walk away, but he had to admit his curiosity was piqued. His wife would probably say he had not been in his right mind in days.

"So, let's say the court gives the Martinez boy possession of the cards," Martin said. "How would your 'encouragement' make those my cards? And what about the kid's father? And the court?"

Wilkins used his index finger to scoop all the snuff out of his mouth and sling it to the ground. He looked up at Martin impatiently.

"We do our work before the court decides the case," Wilkins said plainly. "We make it where you are the only choice they have. We're the ones who put his daddy where he is. I'm sure we could make it where he never comes out, if that's what you need. We got friends in prison."

Martin didn't doubt for a minute that Wilkins had friends serving time. He was also beginning to understand that Randall Wilkins wasn't nearly as dumb as most people in the county thought he was. Ignorant, yes. Dumb, no.

"As for the court, once the Mexicans are out of the way, all we have to do is encourage Judge Lawson to reconsider his original ruling. There won't be anybody left to give them to other than you, and we'll make sure he sees it that way, or we may have to encourage his early retirement."

Martin could not believe what he was hearing from this backwoods bigot, but he kept calm. Randall Wilkins was not afraid to do whatever was necessary to accomplish his goals. And Martin did not want to give Wilkins any reason to put his family on that list.

"So why would you do this for me, Randy? We've never been real enemies, but we're not exactly fishing buddies either," Martin said.

Wilkins turned to the truck, reached through the open window, and grabbed another beer out of the ice chest on the front seat. He used the inside door latch to knock the cap off the bottle and took a long drink.

"Money, of course," he said as if Martin was a complete moron. "What other reason would anybody have?"

"So you're willing to threaten people, or even hurt or kill them, just for a cut of the baseball card money?"

"Bill. Listen to me," Wilkins said in a tired voice. "Killing or hurting Mexicans ain't like hurting or killing regular people. They're stupid and they're lazy. They don't belong here and they got no right to come up here and take things that don't belong to them."

Wilkins held the bottle out, offering Martin a drink. Bill shook his head. He was speechless.

"People talk around here, Bill," Wilkins said. "I know your business is down—way down. I know you're liable to lose it if something doesn't happen quickly. If you want to keep that money where it belongs, and if you're willing to let other people do the hard work for you we can help."

Wilkins climbed back into the truck and slammed the door. He stuck his head out the window. "Well?"

"How much?" Martin asked.

"Half," the former police officer said. "That's all we need to make sure justice is done. Shouldn't be over thirty or forty million dollars. That would still leave you more money that you could ever spend."

Martin stared quietly at the ground where a wet glob of dipping tobacco had landed. The truck roared to life.

"Think about it, Bill," Wilkins said. "But don't think about it too long. Court date's comin' up. And remember, if anyone asks, we never had this conversation."

*****

Police chief Merle Henderson watched the black pickup drive away and then turned to the man seated next to him.

"That the officer you just fired?" the man asked.

"One of them," Chief Henderson said. "That's the one I've heard rumors about for a couple of years now. We've looked at him pretty hard but haven't been able to pin anything on him. He seems stupid when you first meet him, but he's not. He's just smart enough to be dangerous."

"You think he might have had something to do with the bombing of Coberly's car?" the man asked.

"If he didn't actually put the explosive in the car, he knows who did," the chief answered. "The hard part will be proving it."

Both men turned their attention back to the convenience store where a seemingly dazed Bill Martin was slowly climbing into his own truck.

Chief Henderson shook his head.

"Chief, you think that Martin fellow is connected with the bad cop in any way?"

"No," Chief Henderson said. "Bill Martin is kind of a jerk, and maybe a bit of a racist, but I think he's pretty

88

harmless. He may not be the brightest man in the county, but even Bill Martin is not stupid enough to get mixed up with that bunch."

"What do you think that conversation was all about?" the stranger asked, his eyes following Martin as he fumbled to start his truck.

"I don't know, but it must have been something pretty serious because Bill Martin looks like he needs to throw up," the police chief said.

Chapter 14

"So, how's your dad?"

"You don't want to know," Tommy Martin said, drawing circles in the dirt with his finger. "So how's your coach? I still can't believe that umpire attacked him."

"He's a little sore. Has a big bruise on his cheek right below his eye, but I think he'll be fine," Tomás said. "It was pretty crazy, all those adults fighting. Did you see the reports on TV? Man, the whole country must think the people in this town are crazy."

"I think I agree with them," Tommy said with a wry laugh. "I was there and saw it all firsthand. The people in this town *are* crazy."

The boys were sitting on the edge of the grass behind second base at the Little League field at San Moreno City Park. Their feet rested in the red dirt of the infield. They had somehow managed to steer clear of reporters on their way to the park, which was no small feat since the entire county was crawling with camera crews. The sun beat down on them, but a southerly breeze made the Texas afternoon tolerable.

Tomás turned to his friend.

"Can I ask you something, Tommy?"

"Sure," Tommy said. "Anything you want."

"Your dad hates Hispanics, including me, right?"

Tommy thought for a second, not sure how to answer.

"Honest to Pete, I don't really know. I know it seems like he does, but I don't think he was always like this," Tommy finally said. "Granted, he never seemed real happy about us hanging out together, but my mom keeps telling him what good people you and your family are."

A motor roared to life on the adjacent field. Both boys glanced over to see an old man perched on a riding mower, cutting the outfield grass.

"This baseball card thing has made him angry," Tommy said. "I've seen my dad mad a lot. He's the kind of dad who gets angry easy and yells a lot. I know it sometimes scares my mom. Heck, he scares me. But this card thing has made him crazy. It's like he's desperate, and getting those cards is his only hope to survive. I think he sees you as a threat now . . . you're in his way."

Tomás stood, stretching in the afternoon sun. He turned to face Tommy, who was now standing and brushing the dirt off his pants.

"So, do you hate me now, too?" Tomás asked suddenly.

"Do you think I ripped off your father, or made him look bad to the whole world?"

Tommy looked stunned.

"What? No, I don't hate you," he said quickly. "I do wish none of this had happened. I wish my dad hadn't flipped out, and that he wasn't being such a jerk about it."

Tommy stopped and looked at the ground.

"I shouldn't have said that. You know, that part about him being a jerk," Tommy said. "He's my dad, and I love him and I shouldn't call him names."

Tomás slipped his left hand into his baseball glove and held up the ball, offering to play catch. Tommy nodded, pulled his glove on, and scooted back so they were about twenty-five feet apart.

"You're right," Tomás said, tossing the ball to Tommy. "Your dad's not a jerk. He's just really angry for some reason and this gave him a chance to point that anger at somebody. I just wish it wasn't me."

Tommy threw a curve back to Tomás, the ball dipping in the air and moving slightly from right to left, almost like it was on remote control.

"You think he's mad at you? You're lucky you don't live in the same house with him. If you did, he could yell at you constantly about how many millions of dollars we won't get if we lose in court," Tommy said. "That's all he talks about, every minute we're together."

Tomás started to throw the ball back, but stopped halfway through his motion.

"Did you hear?"

"Yeah," Tommy said. "I saw it on the news this morning. The last bid was up to thirty-three million. Can you believe it?"

Tomás shook his head as he threw the ball back.

"That was earlier today," he said. "Mr. Coberly called my mom right before I left to come out here."

This time it was Tommy who stopped his throwing motion halfway through. He looked at Tomás wide-eyed: "How much?"

"Thirty-six million dollars," Tomás muttered so quietly that Tommy could barely hear him.

Tommy dropped the ball. His eyes, as wide as saucers. "You can't be serious."

"That's weird," Tomás said. He stepped close to his friend and scooped the ball off the grass. "That's exactly what my mom said to Mr. Coberly, just before she dropped the phone."

Chapter 15

The principal smiled, but Tomás could tell the man was anything but happy.

"Sit down, Tomás," Mr. Sanders said.

"Is something wrong? Have I done something?" Tomás asked, his voice cracking. He got nervous any time he was called to the office.

"I don't know, Tomás. Have you?" Mr. Sanders asked with the same fake smile. "I can tell you there are a couple of things we need to talk about."

Tomás's stomach turned upside down. "Do I need to call my mom to have her come?"

"That won't be necessary," Mr. Sanders said, waving Tomás toward a chair facing the principal's big desk.

Once Tomás had taken a seat, the principal sat silent for a long time, just looking at Tomás, who fidgeted in his seat. Finally, after what seemed like hours, Mr. Sanders spoke.

"Tomás, have you ever been in trouble here at school with any of your teachers?"

Tomás thought hard, making sure of his answer.

"No sir, not really," Tomás said. "I've been tardy a couple of times, but not really gotten in trouble. I did get a tardy yesterday because I let Hudson Mitchell beat me up out by the lockers."

"Yes," Mr. Sanders said softly. "I heard about that, but that's not quite the story I heard. I heard you started the whole thing by mouthing off to Mr. Mitchell. But we'll come back to that later."

The principal leaned forward, resting his elbows on his desk. "I'm going to be honest with you, Tomás," he said. "I've been told something about you by some other students that I would not normally believe to be true. I am afraid, however, that I don't have any choice but to deal with what I heard."

Tomás's breathing became shallow. He could feel his heart pounding in his chest. His hands and feet went cold and he felt sweat break out on his forehead.

"You heard something about me?" he asked. "Heard what? Heard it from who?"

Mr. Sanders stood and walked around the desk, towering over Tomás. He was a big man and he suddenly seemed much larger to Tomás.

"Do you remember last month when one of our school buses was vandalized?" Mr. Sanders asked abruptly.

"Sure," Tomás said, his fear rising. "I think everybody at school heard about it."

Three weeks earlier over weekend break, someone had broken into the locked bus facility and trashed a school bus. Whoever it was had sprayed the fire extinguisher all through the bus, sliced open most of the seats with a knife, and kicked out a half-dozen windows.

Tomás had a bad feeling where this conversation was going. "I didn't have anything to do with that," Tomás said, jumping up from his chair.

The strong hand of Mr. Sanders eased Tomás back into his seat. "That's not what I've heard from several other students," the principal said. "Some of them said they saw you up here that night. Some others said they heard you bragging yesterday about how you tore up the bus and got away with it."

Tomás couldn't believe what he was hearing. He started shaking his head as he spoke. "No, no!" Tomás yelled suddenly. "That's a lie. Who? Who said these things? Whoever it was, they're lying."

Mr. Sanders still had not let go of Tomás's shoulder. Now his grip tightened. Tomás winced from the pressure.

"Seems like you've been having problems like this a lot lately," the principal said. "You say one thing and somebody else says another. Kind of makes it hard for anyone to trust you, Tomás."

Before Tomás could respond, Mr. Sanders continued.

"There were several witnesses who say they saw you, and their stories all match, Tomás. How can I believe the story of one boy over the word of several other boys?"

"Maybe because all the other boys are lying, and I'm not," Tomás said angrily. "I want to know who said these things. Bring them in here. I want to hear them say it in front of me."

"That's not necessary and it's not going to happen," Mr. Sanders said. "I've already spoken with them one at a time, and they all tell identical stories. They all said they saw you here that night when no one was supposed to be here. And several of them said they heard you in the cafeteria bragging to one of your friends how you were the one who vandalized the bus."

Tomás sat quietly for a moment, his mind racing. *Who would do this to me? I've never had any trouble with any of the kids at school. Why?* Suddenly, he knew the answer.

"Mr. Sanders," he said. "You said they saw me up here that night when no one was supposed to be here?"

"That's right," the principal said. "Several of them saw you."

"If no one was supposed to be here, how did they see me, unless they were here? That would mean they were up here, too. Why were they here?"

"I have no idea," Mr. Sanders said, obviously taken aback. "But nobody saw them around the buses."

"You never said they saw me around the buses," Tomás said. "Is that what they said?"

"The real issue to me," Mr. Sanders said, "is why you were bragging about it to one of your friends if you had nothing to do with it."

"Which friend?" Tomás asked.

"What?"

"Which friend?" he asked again. "If they said they heard me bragging about it to a friend, I want to know which one. It didn't happen. If you bring in whatever friend it was supposed to be, he'll tell you I never said that."

Mr. Sanders removed his hand from Tomás's shoulder, walked back behind his desk, and sat down.

"You think you're pretty smart, don't you Mr. Martinez," the principal said angrily.

"No sir," Tomás replied politely. "But I know when I'm being accused of something I didn't do, and I think I know why."

"Well, Tomás, it really doesn't matter at this point who the friend was, because I'm sure he or she would lie to protect you," Mr. Sanders said.

Tomás stared back at his principal in shock.

"So it doesn't matter that I said I had nothing to do with it, and that you'll never find anyone I know who will say I bragged about it," he said angrily. "That's it? I'm just guilty because *supposedly* some kids came to you and said all this three weeks after it happened?"

Mr. Sanders stood again, anger obvious in his eyes.

"What do you mean some kids 'supposedly' came and said this?" The principal was shouting now.

But Tomás was through being frightened. The principal's reaction told him what he needed to know. He was only twelve years old, but he wasn't stupid. "I said that because you and I both know there are no other kids who said any of those things about me," Tomás said firmly. "You won't tell me who they are because they don't exist, and you won't tell me who the friend was supposed to be because there wasn't any friend.

"You made all this up. I don't know why, but you made all this up, and you're gonna kick me out of school."

The principal looked Tomás squarely in the eye and ignored everything he had just said.

"Mr. Martinez, because of the allegations that have been made and because of information that has been brought to my attention, I have no choice but to suspend you from school until our administrative staff can meet to discuss the matter further," he said coldly. "If we decide these allegations are true—and I have no reason to believe they are not—then you will be expelled from San Moreno Middle School for the remainder of the school year."

Tomás sat quietly as Mr. Sanders pushed a button on his phone. Almost instantly, the door to the office opened, and the school security officer stepped into the room.

"Officer Gray will drive you home, Tomás," Mr. Sanders said. "Your suspension is to begin immediately."

"I won't go," Tomás said flatly.

"Oh you will go, Tomás, or Officer Gray will be forced to take you into custody and lead you out of the school in handcuffs," Mr. Sanders said, failing to hide a slight smile.

Tomás didn't budge, though he could tell the principal wanted him to refuse. "Then I guess he's going to have to get his cuffs out, because I didn't do anything wrong and I'm not going."

The security officer looked to Mr. Sanders, who nodded and motioned to Tomás. The boy stood slowly and stuck his hands out. As the officer was fastening the handcuffs on Tomás's thin wrists, Sam Coberly eased through the door, followed by a livid Juana Martinez.

"Principal Sanders," Coberly said as he approached the desk. "I find it incredible that an administrator with your years of experience would interrogate a twelve-year-old boy on such accusations without his parents present. You didn't even have the courtesy to make a phone call to his parents to inform them of the situation."

Sanders, caught off guard, just stared at Coberly.

"What are you doing here, Sam?" Mr. Sanders asked. "How did you even know . . .?"

He stopped abruptly and glared at Tomás. "Mr. Martinez, are you hiding an illegal cellular device? That would be another violation of school policy."

Tomás smiled, then answered. "No sir, I don't own a cell phone, but some of my friends just might."

"What friends might that be, Tomás?" the principal demanded. Sam Coberly raised his hand to make sure Tomás did not respond.

"Tell you what, Principal Sanders," Coberly said. "You give my client the names of his so-called accusers, and we may consider giving you the names you asked for."

The principal looked stunned.

"Relax, Mr. Sanders," Coberly said. "None of the children called us, but someone else certainly did."

Mr. Sanders glared at the lawyer, the wheels in his

mind churning as he tried to figure out who at the school could have betrayed him.

"You have thin walls and a loud voice, Sanders," the lawyer said. "And I do believe we were met by your secretary as we were coming in the door. She was walking out. She asked us to inform you that her letter of resignation will be in the mail this afternoon."

The principal sat stunned, looking first at Coberly then at Tomás. Coberly again broke the silence.

"Do you want Officer Gray to remove the handcuffs from my client, or do you want me to parade Tomás in handcuffs past two dozen TV reporters as we leave the building?"

"Reporters?"

"Yes, amazing how they show up at exactly the wrong time, or at exactly the right time, depending on your perspective. I've found them to be quite helpful—when used properly," Coberly said with a wink.

Mr. Sanders stood slowly, his face red with anger or humiliation. Tomás couldn't tell for sure which.

"Get out of my office, Coberly."

The lawyer nodded at Tomás, who was holding his arms out. "The cuffs, if you don't mind."

Juana had not spoken since entering the office, but she glared at the principal now as the guard unlocked the handcuffs on her son.

"How dare you try to intimidate a little boy," she spat. "How dare you treat my son like a criminal. What kind of poor excuse for a principal are you?"

She turned without giving the principal a chance to respond, guiding Tomás toward the outer office. Coberly followed, stopping briefly at the door and turning back to face the principal.

"By the way, how is your cousin?"

The principal seemed confused. "What?"

"Your cousin," Coberly said again. "You know, Randall Wilkins, former member of the San Moreno Police Department. How is he handling being unemployed?"

Without waiting for a response, Coberly turned and walked from the room toward the horde of reporters who waited just outside the school's front entrance.

Within three hours, more than one hundred students had been pulled out of San Moreno Middle School by their parents. The common denominator amongst the parents was not race but a shared understanding that children have to be taught to hate and a mutual disgust for the intolerance exhibited by the man with whom they had entrusted their sons and daughters.

By the end of the day, an emergency meeting of the San Moreno School Board had been called for that evening. Principal Riley Sanders, a twenty-seven-year veteran of the district, was not at the meeting held to discuss his employment. Instead, his attorney presented the board with the principal's resignation, in which Mr. Sanders said he was retiring immediately because of poor health.

His secretary, Nancy Johnson, then withdrew her own resignation. She would be back at school the next morning, glad to finally be rid of the man she had tolerated against her better judgment for fourteen years. Neither Tomás nor his attorney attended the meeting, but they heard later that the board unanimously voted to overrule Tomás's suspension, a decision that reportedly drew a chorus of cheers from the audience.

Nothing that transpired at the meeting would have surprised Sam Coberly. He knew most townspeople in San Moreno were good, hardworking people who judged their fellow man by the content of his character not his skin color.

He also knew it only took a few rats to make a place uninhabitable.

But rats like to work in the dark, and so he had not expected them to show up.

Chapter 16

News of Tomás's school suspension and then reinstatement on the false allegations spread like wildfire across the country. The "San Moreno Situation," as one network had begun to call it, was again the lead story on the national evening news. San Antonio investigative TV reporter Brian Singleton somehow learned of the connection between Tomás's principal and the police officer that had investigated the break-in at the Martinez house. When that relationship hit the airwaves, civil rights advocates across the country screamed for an investigation.

Anger boiled over in Hispanic communities from California to Florida, communities all too familiar with having their children treated as Tomás had been. But nowhere did anger run hotter than in Texas, which had become a state in desperate need of calm, thoughtful leadership.

In the Martinez family's own neighborhood, church leaders stepped up to urge patience and restraint. Hispanic preachers appeared at a press conference alongside the white San Moreno mayor. Together they pleaded for calm in the midst of the growing storm and called on the community to begin a process of reconciliation in which all sides would have a chance to voice their grievances and move forward in a positive, productive manner.

Their pleas went mostly ignored.

The situation in San Moreno was like a bottle under pressure too long. The slightest touch was cause enough for it to explode. The unwarranted suspension of Tomás, who had become a beloved celebrity in the barrios of the town, proved to be that trigger.

Two troubled brothers, Lorenzo and Jorge Ortiz, who lived just up the street from the Martinez family, were arrested, charged with vandalism and destruction of property. Before police could corral the two vengeance seekers, the Ortiz brothers went on a rampage. They set fire to a tiny Baptist church building, broke windows at more than a dozen downtown businesses, and slashed the tires on four vehicles belonging to Bill Martin's construction company.

They also ended up in jail.

Meanwhile, the local police switchboard was overwhelmed with calls from both Hispanics and whites about real or perceived slights and wrongs. Chief Henderson had been forced to call in all off-duty officers to keep up with the volume of complaints.

Suspiciously absent from the mayhem were Riley Sanders and Randall Wilkins, though Coberly had a strong hunch the two would resurface in a few days after things had calmed down.

*****

Juana Martinez slipped quietly into the little country church that sat four miles outside San Moreno. She was nervous about her meeting, but the person who had called had seemed genuinely desperate to see her. Juana walked through the foyer and into the sanctuary where she saw a single figure sitting in a pew near the front.

"Mrs. Martin?"

Cindy Martin's head swiveled as she turned to look at Tomás's mother. "Hello, Juana. Thank you for coming."

Juana took a seat in the front pew across from Cindy Martin. The two mothers sat silently for a few moments. Neither seemed able to figure out the best way to begin.

"How is your husband?" Juana finally said.

"About to have a nervous breakdown, but otherwise healthy," Cindy Martin said. "How's yours?"

"In prison for something he didn't do, but otherwise healthy, I guess," Juana Martinez said.

For some reason, both women found this funny and began to chuckle. The chuckles eventually turned into outright laughter that lasted several minutes.

"I'm sorry," Juana said, gasping for breath and wiping tears from her eyes. "I can't believe I'm laughing at my husband being in prison. That's terrible of me—and in church no less."

Cindy Martin was also wiping away tears. "I feel the same way. But I haven't laughed like that in a long time. You know what? It feels good."

Juana nodded, still dabbing at tears with a wad of tissue from her purse. "I haven't laughed since my husband went to prison," she said, offering Mrs. Martin a tissue. "And you're right. It felt very good."

A long silence settled between the two women as they refocused on what had brought them together this day.

"Why did you ask me here?" Juana asked.

"I hoped we might be able to find a way out of this, since none of the men seem to be trying."

Juana took a good look at the mother of her son's best friend. They were about the same age, thirty-something, Juana guessed. Cindy Martin was a bit taller, with long brown hair and sparkling hazel eyes. Juana was petite, with warm brown eyes and a soft voice. Whatever their differences, they were both mothers.

"So, you want me to convince my son and husband to give up the cards or split the money when the court awards the cards to Tomás," Juana said.

It was not really a question. It was more of a statement. It had come out bold, even challenging, though Juana hadn't intended it that way.

"Oh, no," Cindy Martin said. "That would probably be the most reasonable solution to this whole problem. But, I'm sorry to say that my husband probably wouldn't take it if half the proceeds were offered. He is determined to win, at whatever cost."

"Then why are you here?"

"For my son," Cindy Martin said, her voice choking with emotion. "My concern is not over money. I don't care about money. I only care about the relationship between my son and his father. I don't know why, but it has been strained for some time, before this whole baseball card thing came up. That has only made it worse."

She fell silent, wiping a tear from her cheek.

"How can I help?" Juana asked, truly puzzled. She recognized the heartbreak of a mother whose child was hurting, but she saw no solution.

"We all know what Tomás said happened—that Bill told him he could have whatever he found. And we all know what Bill will say—that he told Tomás he could keep whatever he found that was of no value—or something like that," Cindy Martin said.

"Yes," Juana said. "That's what has caused this circus."

Cindy Martin took a deep breath, calming herself.

"And so, what's going to happen is that the court will call Tommy to testify to clear up the whole thing."

Now Juana understood Mrs. Martin's dilemma.

"So, if Tommy tells what he knows his father to have really said, you think it will destroy their relationship for good," Juana offered.

"I don't think it will destroy it," Cindy Martin said, through sobs. "I know it will. If Tommy has to testify, he won't lie, and that means he'll tell the court Bill said Tomás could have whatever he found. If Tommy tells the truth, that means he has to call his own father a liar in front of the whole world. And, if he can't do that, then he has to stand in front of the whole world and testify to something he knows is not the truth. He will have to perjure himself just to protect his father. I can't let that happen. My son is an honest boy."

She stopped again, gathering herself as she turned to face Juana. "Mrs. Martinez, I know you don't really know my husband, but I need you to understand something," Cindy Martin said. "If he says he told Tomás he could keep anything he found, in his mind what he meant was anything of no value. Now granted, one man's trash is another man's treasure, so I am not defending my husband. He should have been much more clear, especially with a twelve-year-old.

"And for the record, I am embarrassed that Bill even offered such a dangerous job to your son. No one's child should have been in that old, dilapidated store working alone. It was wrong. And I hope you will forgive Bill."

"Thank you for admitting that," Juana said quietly.

"As for anything my husband has said about Tomás or your family, as wrong and hurtful as it may have been to you, he never meant any of it. He's losing his business, Mrs. Martinez. He's been losing it for a long time and it's killing him. I think he saw this baseball card thing as the answer to his prayers."

"I do understand, Cindy," Juana said, using Mrs. Martin's first name for the first time. "I know something about the pressure of financial troubles, especially since José went to prison. I appreciate your confiding in me. I know it is not easy to talk about such things. Please know I am so sorry about your family's situation."

The two women fell silent, letting the calm of the little church hold them.

"How is Tommy dealing with all of this?" Juana asked, breaking the silence.

"Not very well," Cindy said softly. "He's staying at his grandmother's house for now because he can't bear facing his father's anger. He doesn't know what to do, and I don't know how to help him."

She took a deep breath, fighting back the tears again.

"He's only twelve, Juana. He shouldn't have to face decisions like this with the whole world watching."

Juana stood softly and stepped across the aisle, taking Cindy Martin's hand in hers.

"Then I think our prayer should be that he doesn't have to make that choice in front of the whole world," she said.

Cindy Martin looked up through her tears and saw Juana smiling reassuringly at her before turning and walking slowly back up the aisle and out the door into the night.

Chapter 17

Sam Coberly glanced quickly behind him and knocked on the hotel room door. After a moment's delay, the door opened a crack and Juana Martinez looked out.

"I need to talk with you and Tomás," Coberly said. "Something's happened to José."

The door closed, and Coberly heard Juana unfastening the inside safety chain. She jerked the door open and looked at her lawyer with terror in her eyes.

"Is he okay? Please tell me he's okay."

Coberly stepped into the room, shutting the door behind him. Tomás had been sitting on the bed on the far side of the room, but now jumped off in Coberly's direction. "Is my father okay, Mr. Coberly?"

Sam nodded. "He's okay," the lawyer said quietly. "He's been attacked, but except for some bumps and bruises he is fine, from what I have been told. He is a lucky man."

"Attacked?" Juana said in alarm. "Why? By whom? How could that happen with so many guards around?"

Sam Coberly moved toward the small table by the wall. He pulled one chair out for Juana and then sat in the other.

"There's a lot I don't know about what happened," he said. "But, from what I was told, it's entirely possible that it may have been a guard or several guards that attacked your husband."

Juana closed her eyes, folded her arms on the table, and laid down her head. "When will it stop?" she whispered.

"Now, now, let's focus on the positives. José is okay," Sam reassured her. "He's been moved to another location, and he's safe for now. They think his nose may be broken, and perhaps his jaw. He was attacked in his cell by at least two men, and some of the inmates are saying it was the work of some guards."

"Why would guards hurt my father?" Tomás asked.

Sam didn't answer immediately. He seemed to think about the question for a long time.

"It was about the cards," Coberly said quietly.

"The cards? Why would they hurt my father over some baseball cards? They won't get the cards or the money, even if the court rules against us."

Coberly turned his chair to address Tomás. "From what the other prisoners said, all the while the guards were beating your father they kept telling him to drop the fight over the cards."

"But why? How does that help them?"

"My guess," Coberly began, "is that they are working for someone here locally. I think this local person hopes to get at least part of the money if you all quit fighting and the cards are awarded to Mr. Martin."

Tomás's anger flared.

"So Tommy's dad had this done to my father, or someone who works for Tommy's dad?"

Juana reached out a hand to calm her son. "That's ridiculous, Mr. Coberly," she said. "I don't believe Mr. Martin would do that, and I don't think you do either."

Coberly took Juana's hand in his. "Remember, Mrs. Martinez, you're talking about an awful lot of money—at this point in excess of forty million dollars. That kind of money could make almost anyone act a little crazier than normal," he said.

Juana pulled her hand away. "Sam, this is not people acting crazy. This is pure greed. And it is wrong," Juana said. "This is the police, the school principal, and now the guards in prison—the very people we trust to protect those in their care and to treat everyone equally—abdicating their responsibility. If you can't trust the police or a school principal to be fair, America will not long be a safe place to raise a family."

Coberly began to clap.

"Well said, Juana. I am embarrassed to say that I let dollar signs cloud my own eyes for a minute."

Juana smiled, stood, and put her arm around Tomás's shoulder. Her face turned grave.

"Is it still worth it, Tomás?" she asked. "Is the money worth all this?"

"It's not just about the money, Mama," Tomás said. "Mr. Martin has called me a liar and a thief. If I give up now, I can't prove that I am not those things."

"But you know you are not those things," Juana said. "If we keep trying to prove it just to save our honor, someone could get hurt or killed. That is something we would have to carry on our conscience for the rest of our lives."

Tomás sat on the edge of the bed, twisting his hands in his lap.

"We have to stand up for our family name," he said. "I know we don't need millions of dollars. Nobody needs that much money. But we have to have some of that money to hire a new lawyer, like Mr. Coberly, to prove Father's innocence. We have to keep fighting—even if we give away most of the money when this whole thing is done. We can't quit. We just can't."

He was crying when he finished, but he stood and embraced his mother. They wept together for several minutes. Sam Coberly stood by respectfully, letting Juana and Tomás shed some of the emotional energy they had kept bottled up inside for so long.

"Let's go see José," Sam said finally. "I think he could use a friendly face about this time, and I think we could all use some time away from this town."

Chapter 18

That night found Bill Martin walking a lonely country road in the middle of nowhere. He hated walking, but he had no other option. He had called a wrecker for his truck after the Ortiz brothers had slashed all the tires. Marion Crabtree had hauled the pickup into town, but said the tires couldn't be replaced until the next morning.

What Bill Martin needed to do couldn't wait until tomorrow, so he had put on his boots and headed out the door just after eight o'clock. He headed northeast toward in-laws' farm.

The day before, Tommy had gone to stay with Cindy's mother and father. The stress of the baseball card dispute was driving the whole Martin family crazy. Cindy Martin had felt it would be best if Tommy and his father had some time apart.

Earlier that day, Bill's wife had joined their son. When she left, she told Bill it was only until the court case was over. She promised they would all be together again when things settled down. Bill wasn't sure he believed her, but he hoped she meant what she said.

After buying a new cell phone to replace the one he had destroyed the night the baseball mess had begun, Bill called his in-laws. Cindy wouldn't talk to him, and nobody in the house would call Tommy to the phone. That was when he had decided to go see them in person.

It was an eight-mile trip to the farm, and Bill's arthritic knees screamed in pain with every step. And that wasn't the worst of it. He had been honked at by at least three passing pickups, endured slurs from several motorists, and been chased by two dogs. It was hard to run on two bad knees, but he had managed to get away from the dogs. Finally, mercifully, he saw the mailbox. He turned off the highway and limped up the drive to the two-story farmhouse.

He knew he wouldn't be welcome at the front door, so he had to find another way to talk to Tommy. He needed desperately to talk with his son. There were some things he had to say. Things he should never have had to say at all, but things he certainly should have said before now.

*****

Tommy lay on the bed in what had once been the bedroom belonging to Shawn, his mother's younger brother.

Shawn was thirty-three now and lived near Waco. Looking out the second floor window, Tommy could see the moon, nearly full, sliding across the nighttime Texas sky.

Then he saw something that nearly made him scream. But before he could yell for help he started laughing instead.

His father sat perched on a limb just beyond the window, twenty feet up in the old elm tree that grew beside the house. It appeared Bill Martin had climbed until he was level with the bedroom window and then inched his way out onto the tree branch. If he reached out as far as possible, it looked like he could maybe tap the glass without falling . . . As his dad stretched to do just that, Tommy raised the window.

"Dad? What in the world are you doing? You'll kill yourself."

Bill Martin was deathly afraid of heights. He smiled weakly, trying to reassure himself and his son that he would, indeed, not kill himself.

"I need to talk," he told his son. "Since they won't let you come to the phone, I figured this was the next best thing."

"Dad," Tommy said. "I didn't want to leave home, but you were so mad, and Mom said it would be best."

"It's okay, Tommy," his dad said. "I understand. It's not your fault."

"It's not? You acted like it was. You were so angry with me, and I am so confused about what I should do. Whatever I do, it is going to hurt somebody," Tommy said.

Sitting twenty feet up in a tree outside a window in the dark of the night, Bill Martin felt more like an idiot than an adult. But some things needed to be said and they needed to be said before morning. *It's time for me to start acting like a grown-up.*

"I know," he said. "And I hate that, Tommy, more than you know. I'm really not angry with you. And believe it or not, I don't hate that Martinez kid."

Tommy rolled his eyes.

"His name is Tomás, Dad. And he isn't just a kid—he's my best friend."

"Okay, okay, I don't hate your friend Tomás. Is that better?"

Bill Martin closed his eyes and shook his head, angry with himself.

"Tommy, I'm sorry. It's not him and it's not you." He held onto the limb tightly with both hands, glancing nervously down into the darkness below him. "I have been under so much pressure. I'm still under pressure. I'm about to lose everything we have. Do you understand how much it hurts for a man to realize he's a failure as a husband, as a father, and as a businessman, all at the same time? Do you?"

Tommy reached for his dad, but he was too far away.

"You're not a failure, Dad."

"Yeah, I have been, but I can change that if you and your mom will just give me a chance."

Bill Martin's eyes filled with tears. Tommy couldn't believe what he was seeing. He had never seen his father cry.

"You okay, Dad?"

Bill Martin nodded, and then slowly repositioned himself on the limb and reached inside his shirt pocket.

"Here, Tommy, I have something I want you to give to that lawyer, Sam Coberly. It's very important, so you have to make sure he gets it."

Tommy reached out his hand—but before his dad could make the handoff his eyes went wide in surprise. Tommy heard a crack and watched as his father plunged into the darkness below, striking the ground with a terrible thud.

Chapter 19

The large courtroom in the San Moreno County Courthouse was a very big room, but in the end it wasn't anywhere near big enough. Three hundred people filled the benches and lined the back and side walls. Three times that many would have squeezed in if they could. It seemed all of Texas and half of the world wanted a ticket to watch the case of *Martin v. Martinez*.

The Martinez case was the first in the courthouse's long and colorful history to require an overflow location. Judge Franklin Lawson had arranged for a live video feed to be broadcast on a giant screen in the high school gymnasium two blocks away. That was the best he could do, but it wasn't good enough. Most of those who failed to get an actual seat in the courthouse would never vote for Lawson again.

A lottery drawing was held for the two hundred public seats available. Half of the seats in that lot—also awarded by lottery drawing—were reserved for the media. The remaining hundred or so seats were quickly snatched up by community leaders, local lawyers, and courthouse workers.

A blinding Texas sun shone on Judge Lawson as he walked the two blocks from his house to the courthouse the morning of the hearing. While it was a short walk, he normally drove to work—thanks to an old injury that tended to give him back spasms. But today he decided to ignore the pain so he could enjoy the attention of the mob of reporters who would be waiting outside the courthouse.

He was not disappointed.

Reporters and photographers surged toward the judge the moment he turned the corner on the last leg of his trip. He appeared to shy away from them at first, but any sharp observer would have recognized that he was more than happy to interrupt his walk when the television camera lights came on. He might pretend to be bothered by the attention, but he appeared thrilled to have a chance to offer his take on what he expected to happen when the hearing started in a little more than an hour.

Judge Lawson was an old man who had never been on television before, who had never presided over the kind of trial that guaranteed free drinks at the local watering hole for life. This was his shot to remedy that. The thought of having his comments broadcast live to a nationwide—if not worldwide—audience was the most exciting thing that had ever happened to him.

Judge Lawson cleared his throat and donned his most authoritative voice.

"I can't, of course, comment on the case itself, or the merits of either of the claims involved," he said majestically. "But I can tell you that this court will, of course, act in the best interest of all parties involved. We will uphold all the laws of this county, the great state of Texas, and, of course, the Constitution of these United States of America."

As the judge finished his carefully prepared and rehearsed speech for the cameras, he realized he had already lost the reporters' attention.

Bill Martin and his attorney had stepped out of an SUV in front of the red-bricked courthouse. They were now being mobbed by the very same reporters who just minutes before had been hanging on the judge's every word. Both men refused comment and fought their way up the steps and into the safety of the building.

Sam Coberly, walking beside Juana and Tomás, did not disappoint the press when his group arrived moments later. The attorney paused, making sure each and every member of the media had an opportunity to focus a camera on him. He then smiled, basking in the glorious morning sunshine, and in their attention.

"On behalf of Juana and Tomás Martinez, my clients in this landmark case, I want to thank you for your coverage of the events of the past few weeks," he said in his best Perry Mason voice. "In the matter of an hour or so, I fully expect this court to show its wisdom by awarding my clients legal custody of the items in dispute—that being the six cases of unopened, factory-sealed, mint condition 1952 Topps baseball cards."

Chapter 20

Judge Franklin Lawson brought the wooden gavel down hard on his bench, sending a loud "crack" through the packed courtroom.

"This court will come to order," he said in his gravelly voice. He waited for the murmur of three hundred people to die away before he continued. "The case of *Martin v. Martinez* will now be heard. Are both sides prepared to proceed?"

Sam stood first, Juana and Tomás seated next to him at the table on the judge's left. "We are ready, Your Honor."

Next, Mark Wallis stood at the table to the judge's right, where he was joined by Bill Martin. Wallis's client had a new cast on his right arm from the shoulder to the wrist. Martin also had bruises on his right cheek and his forehead. He looked as if he had been run over by a truck.

"We are ready as well, Your Honor," Wallis said.

The judge took a moment to admire Bill Martin's cast, then brought the gavel down again on the bench.

"Mr. Coberly, let's get this show on the road," he said firmly. "Please call your first witness."

Sam Coberly stood again and turned to look out over those seated behind him in the public gallery. "We call Tommy Martin to the stand, Your Honor."

Mark Wallis leaned over to whisper to his client: "He sure didn't waste any time, did he?"

"That's Sam," Martin said. "If there's anything he can do to ruin my day, he does it in a hurry. I never have liked that man very much, but he is a good lawyer."

Another wave of murmuring rolled through the courtroom as every head turned to find Bill Martin's son in the crowd. He was near the back of the gallery, sitting on the aisle next to his mother. Cindy Martin held her son's hand as he stood, but she was glaring at her husband.

Tommy wobbled on shaky legs, moving at a snail's pace. He was not in a hurry to take the witness stand. He would rather go to bat blindfolded against a Major League pitcher than sit in that witness chair. His mother held his hand until he finally pulled away and began the slow march up the aisle to the witness chair.

The audience was dead silent. Tommy was halfway through the gallery when a deep voice came from the front of the courtroom.

"Your Honor, may I speak first?" Bill Martin was standing at his table.

Judge Lawson, who had been making notes on a legal pad, looked up quickly.

"Is there a problem, Mr. Martin?"

"Several, Your Honor," Martin said. He stood slowly, grimacing with pain. "But I don't think the court wants to hear about them all. May I speak?"

Tommy stood in the middle of the aisle, not sure what he was supposed to do.

"Is it truly necessary that we interrupt the proceedings before they even begin, Mr. Martin?" the judge asked in obvious irritation.

"It's more necessary than you can imagine, Your Honor," Martin said. "I believe if you allow me to speak for just a moment, it may not be necessary to continue the hearing at all."

Judge Lawson looked both puzzled and disappointed but also intrigued. "That sounds very interesting, Mr. Martin. You may speak. Tommy Martin, you may be seated again for the time being."

Tommy heaved an enormous sigh of relief and nearly ran back to his seat, plopping down next to his mother. All eyes focused on Tommy's father, who looked like he would rather be anywhere else in the world besides this particular courtroom.

Bill Martin stood alone, gathering his courage. He had a mortal fear of public speaking. He could feel every set of eyes boring into him as the entire courtroom waited to hear what he had to say. He turned to glance at the packed gallery and then looked across at the table where

Juana and Tomás Martinez sat with Sam Coberly. He then turned slowly back to the judge.

After a long pause, his shoulders drooped noticeably. He took a deep breath, let it out slowly, and finally managed to say the words he had been practicing for the past few hours.

"Your Honor, I don't want the cards."

Judge Lawson's mouth fell open as he stared unbelievingly at the man in the cast.

"Excuse me, Mr. Martin?"

"I said I do not want the cards, Your Honor," Martin repeated, his voice more firm this time.

"I heard you the first time, Mr. Martin," the judge said angrily. "I just wanted to make sure you knew what you were saying because I thought that was the reason we were all here in the first place."

Martin ignored the judge's remark and turned to look at Tomás Martinez, whose mouth was hanging open in disbelief.

"They are his cards, Your Honor," Martin said, still looking at Tomás. "I told him he could keep whatever he found in that old building, and he found those cards. He kept his part of the agreement, and now it's time I kept mine."

He stopped talking for a few seconds and then looked at Juana Martinez, who was staring at him as if he had grown three heads.

"All I ask is that the Martinez family loan me enough money out of the sale of those cards to get my business back on track. I also ask that they then let me pay back that loan—with interest, Your Honor."

Judge Lawson threw up his hands and looked at Martin's lawyer. Mark Wallis shrugged his shoulders in response. He had no idea what was going on.

"Your Honor, for the record, my client has apparently lost his mind," Wallis said. "This is certainly not something we have discussed, so I have no idea why he just said what he did or what he might say next."

Across the aisle, Juana Martinez turned from talking with her son. She tugged on Sam Coberly's jacket sleeve and then whispered in his ear. The two adults carried on a brief conversation before the lawyer stood slowly and addressed the judge.

"Your Honor, my client has just informed me that she and her family have also decided that they do not want the cards," Coberly announced to the court.

Judge Lawson sat back suddenly in his chair as if he'd been slapped. The crowd erupted with nervous laughter, but stopped abruptly when the judge began banging his gavel for silence.

"Are you serious, Mr. Coberly?" he asked in amazement.

"As serious as a broken arm," Coberly said with a smile, looking at Bill Martin.

"Funny, Sam," Martin said, wincing in pain. "Very, very funny."

Judge Lawson glared at Sam Coberly, then glared at Bill Martin. He started to speak but stopped, only to glare at both men again for an uncomfortable amount of time.

"Doesn't anybody want these cards?" the judge asked.

Several hands shot up around the courtroom. They went back down quickly when Judge Lawson slammed his gavel down again and proceeded to glare out across the audience. Heaving a big sigh, the judge proceeded to sternly confront Bill Martin and Sam Coberly.

"Let me get this straight, gentlemen," he said slowly. "Up for grabs are six cases of extremely valuable and very rare baseball cards that I believe could sell at this very moment for more than fifty million dollars. Do I have that right?"

Coberly knew someone should answer the judge; he just didn't want it to be him. But after a brief pause, he answered for both men. "That's correct, Your Honor."

This time the judge spoke only to Bill Martin. "Yet we were all summoned here today, and the state has spent a great deal of money in preparing to hear this case because both sides were determined to win custody of these same cards? Is that right, Mr. Martin?"

"That is also correct, Your Honor," Martin said in a shaky voice.

Judge Lawson took a deep breath, chewing on his bottom lip before continuing his address: "And, if I'm not mistaken, it was you, Mr. Martin, who actually filed the lawsuit that brought us all together this morning. Am I correct?"

Now it was Bill Martin's turn to squirm. He shifted from one foot to the other, staring at the floor.

"Mr. Martin?"

"Yes, Your Honor," Martin said so quietly that hardly anyone could hear him.

"A little louder, Mr. Martin," Judge Lawson said firmly.

"Yes, sir," Bill Martin said clearly. "I was the one who filed the legal challenge for ownership of the cards."

The judge sat back in his chair, nodding his head and pointing at both Bill Martin and Sam Coberly.

"And yet, suddenly, for whatever reason, you've both had a change of heart, and now nobody wants these cards," the judge said flatly. "You all have changed your minds about something that for weeks has been all you could talk about, and we're all just supposed to pack up and go home?"

He waited for an answer, but neither Coberly nor Martin responded.

"Well gentlemen, I have to say I'm actually rather proud of both sides. I am also more surprised than you will ever know," the judge said. "But I still have one tremendous legal problem on my hands. What am I supposed to do with fifty million dollars worth of rare baseball cards that nobody wants and that—according to the law—nobody owns right now?"

Bill Martin looked lost as he stood motionless before the judge. Sam Coberly thought for a moment, and then raised his hand like a seventh-grade student hoping to be called on by his teacher.

"Your Honor, if I might point something out?"

"Please, Mr. Coberly. I would be delighted to hear someone say something that would begin to make sense of all of this," the judge replied. "I, myself, am completely flummoxed at this turn of events."

Mr. Coberly nodded in understanding—he had almost suffered whiplash from how fast the case had turned.

"Your Honor, the legal issue at hand, I believe, was whether or not Mr. Martin had told my client that he could keep anything he found in that old building. Am I correct?"

"That is correct, Mr. Coberly," the judge said. "Again, that is why we are all here."

"Well, Your Honor, I believe legal ownership of the cards was decided when Mr. Martin stood before this court and admitted that he had told Tomás Martinez that he could, in fact, keep anything he found when he cleaned out that building. Is that not what you just told us, Mr. Martin?"

"Yes, Sam. That's what I said," Bill Martin answered. "Those are Tomás's cards, or his and his mother's."

Judge Lawson shot a look at Bill Martin.

"So, Mr. Martin. You've suddenly found your voice again, I see," the judge said.

Before Martin could answer, the back doors into the courtroom opened and Police Chief Merle Henderson strolled up the aisle. He leaned over the waist-high railing dividing the spectators from the lawyers and held a brief whispered conversation with Sam Coberly.

The lawyer then stood to address Judge Lawson as the police chief walked back down the aisle and out of the courtroom.

"Your Honor, would there be any possible way we could request a bailiff to bring us another chair?"

The judge sighed deeply and rolled his eyes.

"Mr. Coberly, I'm growing weary of these proceedings. Why would you have need of another chair? Are your bunions bothering you again? Do you have need to elevate that old leg of yours?"

Sam Coberly smiled broadly at Juana and Tomás.

"No Your Honor, but José Martinez has just arrived, and I am certain he would want to sit with his wife and his son while we work this out."

Chapter 21

Two minutes later, the entire Martinez family had joined Coberly at the defendant's table. Juana wiped the tears from her face, while Tomás beamed the biggest smile Tommy Martin had ever seen on his friend's face—bigger, even, than the time Tomás hit a home run in the league championship.

José Martinez, his nose still badly swollen from his prison beating, was nonetheless beaming, too. He looked terrible and in pain, but you couldn't tell it from his smile. He seemed to be having the time of his life.

Police Chief Merle Henderson, who had accompanied José into the courtroom, now stood quietly before Judge Lawson.

"Mr. Coberly, Mr. Wallis, please approach the bench," the judge ordered.

Once the two lawyers had joined the police chief, Lawson nodded toward Chief Henderson.

"Gentlemen, there are a lot of questions I need answered, and I don't believe open court is the best place to take care of that," Judge Lawson said. "Why don't we take a fifteen-minute recess, and then you can all join me in my chambers where we can figure out what in the world is going on."

"Your Honor, can we bring in our clients?" Wallis asked. "I think the entire process would go more smoothly if everyone involved was able to take part in this conversation."

"It's a small office, Mr. Wallis, but I am willing to do whatever it takes to get through this, if you are," said the judge.

When Judge Lawson pounded the gavel on the bench and called for a recess, the crowd sounded a collective gasp of disappointment.

*****

Three minutes later, Judge Lawson's chamber was filled to capacity.

Wallis and Bill Martin were joined by José and Juana, Tomás Martinez and Sam Coberly. Chief Henderson stood awkwardly to the side as the judge burst into the room and took a seat behind his desk.

"I'd ask everyone to please be seated, but there simply aren't enough chairs in here," Judge Lawson said. "So stand, or sit, or lean on a desk or something so we can get through this and get back into that courtroom."

Judge Lawson opened his notebook, picked up a silver ink pen, and looked at the police chief.

"Now, Chief Henderson, since things were stumbling along pretty well until you arrived on the scene with Mr. Martinez, why don't we start with you."

"Your Honor, we received information last night that Mr. Martin had taped a conversation a few days ago between himself and one of my former officers," the chief began.

"Would that be with a Mr. Wilkins?" the judge asked sarcastically.

"Yes, sir, it would," Chief Henderson answered. "Randall Wilkins, who is no longer employed by the city and who has turned in his badge at my request—that same Randall Wilkins is now missing and a warrant has been issued for his arrest. On this tape, Mr. Wilkins can be heard taking credit for the assault on José Martinez while Mr. Martinez was incarcerated in the state penitentiary."

Judge Lawson looked at José Martinez, his face bruised and battered.

"Go on," the judge said.

"Mr. Wilkins goes on to say on the tape that he had contacted two guards at the prison who belong to a hate group of which Mr. Wilkins is also a member. Randall Wilkins convinced those guards to beat Mr. Martinez in an attempt to frighten or kill him. His objective was to convince the other members of the Martinez family to give up their fight for the baseball cards and allow Bill Martin to be awarded ownership in court," Chief Henderson said.

The judge looked confused.

"I don't understand," Judge Lawson said. "Even if that all took place, how would that benefit Mr. Wilkins and his . . . friends?"

Bill Martin stepped forward hesitantly.

"If I may speak, Your Honor? I think I can shed some light on that."

The judge nodded. "Go ahead, Bill."

"Randy approached me with this idea first at the gas station the day after the cards were found, but I told him I was not interested. He came back to me a second time—when I made this recording—and told me they were going to go through with it anyway. Only this time they threatened me, too. He said when José Martinez was out of the picture, and I was awarded the cards, if I didn't give them half of whatever money I won, they would kill my family," Martin said.

"I see," Judge Lawson said quietly. "It seems Mr. Wilkins is a bit more ambitious than a lot of us realized."

Chief Henderson glanced at José Martinez and gestured for permission to speak.

Again the judge nodded.

"That's not all, Your Honor," the police chief said. "Mr. Wilkins can also be heard on this tape telling Mr. Martin that he and his brother, Charlie Wilkins, framed Mr. Martinez for the theft of several thousand dollars from a local lumber company a year ago."

"I remember that case," Judge Lawson said. "That was supposed to come before my court, but as I remember it, Mr. Martinez's attorney entered a plea of no contest on his behalf."

"That's correct, Your Honor," Mr. Coberly interrupted. "Mr. Martinez was convinced by his attorney that a plea of no contest would be better for his family than taking the case to trial. Mr. Martinez's attorney assured him that he would receive a suspended sentence, or probation. We now know that attorney had also been compromised by Mr. Wilkins and his associates."

Judge Lawson muttered something under his breath and made a few quick notes on his legal pad. He turned back to Chief Henderson so the police chief could finish.

"According to what Randall Wilkins says on the tape, his brother was the one who actually took the money from the lumber yard, and then blamed it on Mr. Martinez," Chief Henderson said. "The Wilkinses were betting that locals here would take the word of a white man over the word of a Hispanic man in such a matter, Your Honor."

Judge Lawson snorted.

"A travesty of assumptions, Chief Henderson," the judge said. "I may not be able to change how racist jurors vote, but that does not make it right. And it is why our system of justice allows for an appeal of a verdict, though that does a man with a bad attorney little good, I'm afraid."

"That's the reason Mr. Martinez has been in prison for the past several months," Chief Henderson said. "Witnesses lied and the jury believed them. And his attorney was incompetent. It's now become clear that Mr. Martinez is, in fact, innocent of all charges pertaining to the embezzlement. Our recommendation would be to bring Mr. Martinez into court and publicly announce that he has been exonerated of all charges, Your Honor."

Judge Lawson hesitated before responding. This was all a little unconventional. But then he made up his mind.

"Mr. Martinez, I am afraid that there is nothing I can do to give you back the months you lost in prison and away from your family," Judge Lawson said. "But I would be more than happy to be the one to announce to the people of this county that you have been found not guilty in regard to the embezzlement charges and that you will, from this moment on, be a free man."

With those words, José pulled his wife into a close hug as Juana began to weep with joy. Tomás joined their embrace, and everyone in the room smiled as the family rejoiced. José was the first to break the moment.

"Thank you, Your Honor," he said.

"I only wish I could do more, Mr. Martinez," the judge said, and his voice was tinged with regret.

Sam Coberly stepped forward. An astute observer would have noticed that the old lawyer was twirling his thumbs again.

"Maybe you can, Your Honor," Coberly said. "I turned over to both the local police and the FBI a copy of that audiotape provided to me at the hospital last night by Mr. Bill Martin. As Chief Henderson stated, on that tape is the voice of Randall Wilkins, the former member of our esteemed police department. Your Honor, it would seem that Mr. Wilkins also offered his talents of persuasion to help convince various people in positions of authority—yourself included—that this court should award custody of those cards to Mr. Martin."

Coberly stopped for a moment to allow the judge to absorb what he had just revealed.

It only took a second.

The judge, visibly angry now, addressed Coberly.

"When you say 'talents,' what exactly do you mean?"

"He admitted his attempts—and the attempts of several of his colleagues—to first intimidate the Martinez family by ransacking and vandalizing their home, and then roughing up José in prison," Coberly explained. "He and his buddies knew both would make headlines. It appears they intended to send a warning to any other potential witnesses who might have ideas about coming forward to testify on behalf of the Martinez family. And the tape also makes it very clear that they intended to bring their efforts into the courthouse if need be."

Coberly stopped again, wanting to be careful about how he approached what he had to say next.

"He went so far, Your Honor, as to tell Mr. Martin that he—Mr. Wilkins—would do whatever was necessary to convince you to rule in favor of the Martins, even if that meant he had to eliminate you," the lawyer said.

Judge Lawson's eyes lit up.

"He was going to have me *eliminated?*" the judge asked in amazement. "He said that on tape?"

"Yes, Your Honor," Coberly said. "He said it more than once. And, yes, we have it on tape."

Judge Lawson laughed out loud. "I'm going to have to listen to that recording, Mr. Coberly. I find it more than a little interesting that someone the likes of Mr. Wilkins believes I am so all-fired important that I might need to be eliminated.

"Chief Henderson," the judge said, "I believe you know what this means."

"Yes, Your Honor," the police chief said, "I'll have my men bring him in."

Chapter 22

Ten minutes later José Martinez stood in front of a San Moreno District Court judge for the second time in his life. The last time, he had been a broken man, unjustly accused and sentenced to prison for stealing money from his employer.

But this time, with his wife and son watching proudly from the defendant's table, he smiled broadly as he listened to the judge render his decision.

"José Martinez," the judge began. "Through further investigation by members of our local law enforcement departments, it has been determined that you were framed for the crime for which you were sent to prison. I deeply apologize to you on behalf of this court, this county, and the state of Texas. You are, Mr. Martinez, a free man. You are free to go."

Juana Martinez bounded from her chair, with Tomás right behind her. As José turned, his wife and son threw their arms around him—the sound of their sobbing filled the courtroom as the family celebrated José's release and the three of them being back together free to resume their normal lives.

"Mr. Martinez, if you would please escort your family back to the defendant's table, we'll continue with our hearing," Judge Lawson said.

Hand in hand, Juana and José walked to the table as Sam Coberly grabbed the extra chair for José. The judge then turned his attention to the two groups sitting at the opposing tables in front of him. Shaking his head in disbelief, Judge Lawson looked out at his packed courtroom and then spoke quietly but firmly.

"This has been one of the most interesting cases I have ever presided over," he said. "And I do not take lightly the responsibility of deciding which of these two families will take ownership of millions of dollars worth of rare baseball cards and which family will go away empty-handed. And, because of that, I want to thank the Martin and Martinez families for meeting with me in chambers so that we could arrive at the best possible solution, one that would be acceptable to all parties involved."

The judge paused for several seconds as the standing-room-only crowd sat stone still waiting to hear his decision.

"In the case of *Martin v. Martinez*, I hereby award possession of the San Moreno Baseball Cards to . . . Mr. Sam

Coberly," Judge Lawson announced, a wide smile spreading across his face.

Gasps erupted around the courtroom as Sam Coberly dropped back into his chair, his mouth hanging open. For several moments he was speechless, and then he managed a simple question.

"Me?"

"That's right, Sam," Judge Lawson said. "And, if my information is correct, the latest bid is somewhere in the neighborhood of fifty million dollars, give or take a few thousand. That means, Mr. Coberly, when that auction ends in three days, you will immediately take possession of at least fifty million dollars."

Coberly coughed, his eyes wide. At the plaintiff's table, Bill Martin chuckled.

"But my decision does come with some stipulations, Mr. Coberly," the judge added. "As a requirement of this decision, you are to award five million dollars to both the Martin and the Martinez families. Do you understand?"

Coberly gathered himself and sat up in his chair. "Yes, Your Honor. I understand."

Coberly paused after that, thought about what he had just said, and changed his mind. "No, sir. To be honest, Your Honor, I don't really understand any of this."

The judge ignored Coberly and continued.

"And, since the total revenue from the sale of the cards is expected to be about fifty million dollars, you will then place another thirty-five million dollars into a special trust fund over which you are to be one of five trustees. The purpose of this fund will be to support a variety of charities both in Texas and other places where this group of trustees feel there is a significant financial need."

Coberly stood slowly, raising his hand in an attempt to be given permission to speak.

"Your Honor, that still leaves approximately five million dollars unaccounted for," the lawyer said.

"I know that, Sam," the judge answered quickly. "I'm not stupid."

"No, Your Honor," Coberly said quietly, sitting back in his chair. "No, you're not."

Judge Lawson took his glasses off and continued.

"You are hereby ordered to set aside two million dollars each for Tomás Martinez and Tommy Martin, with the stipulation that neither of those two accounts is to be accessed until the boys are eighteen years of age."

Judge Lawson stopped and eyed Coberly. He could tell the lawyer was dying to point out that this still left one million dollars unaccounted for, but Sam knew better than to say anything. The judge, on the other hand, also knew Coberly was going crazy trying to figure out where the other million dollars was going to go.

"Mr. Coberly," he said finally. "How much money do we have left over?"

Coberly frowned as if it were a trick question.

"I believe we still have a million dollars, Your Honor," the lawyer answered hesitantly.

The judge smiled at Coberly. "Then, as they say in the restaurant business, keep the change, Sam."

Coberly dropped his ink pen and stared blankly at his old friend behind the bench.

"Excuse me, Your Honor?"

"It's yours, Mr. Coberly, at the request of both families involved in this case. They wanted to give you more—I think the number was ten million—for your assistance in helping us all to reach an amicable resolution to this case. But, having known you for nearly fifty years, I knew giving you that much money would make you impossible to live with. So, you'll have to settle for the million dollars, minus some for taxes, of course," Judge Lawson said.

For the first time in his life, Sam Coberly was speechless. He threw up his hands and sat down hard in his chair, laughing until he cried. As a lawyer who represented the poor and disenfranchised, Sam Coberly had expected to die a pauper.

Chapter 23

Bill Martin could not believe what he was seeing. The legendary rock-and-roll group ZZ Top was playing live in downtown San Moreno and more than twenty thousand people had packed the town square for the community's annual End of Summer celebration. The event normally drew no more than a few thousand people, but like so many things in San Moreno it was on the upswing.

"Hey, Dad, who are these guys again? They're not half bad."

Martin looked down at Tommy, who was stuffing the last two bites of a hot dog into his mouth.

"You're not serious," Martin said to his son.

"Are they new?" Tommy asked, his words barely intelligible because of all the food in his mouth.

"You are serious," Martin said shaking his head. "We're

going to have to work on your pop culture references."

Before Tommy could ask his dad to explain what pop culture was, he spotted Tomás Martinez a few yards up the street talking with a group of friends.

"I'll be right back, Dad." He was off in a flash. Seconds later, he was fully absorbed in a conversation with Tomás and several classmates.

Watching the two boys give each other a high five, Martin thought back over the events of the past few weeks. It was difficult to believe how fast life could change.

The prison guards who had assaulted José had been arrested and had confessed to their association with Randall Wilkins and the racist group that had been threatening folks in the San Moreno area. Wilkins had been found and arrested and was now residing in the county jail. He was awaiting trial on a long list of charges, including conspiracy to commit murder against an officer of the court, aggravated assault, intimidation of a witness, and a number of civil rights violations. Riley Sanders, the former middle school principal, had moved to Iowa to live with his elderly mother. Before leaving town, he had written an apology to the Martinez family and the community.

It had taken awhile for the media circus to pull up its tent after the court hearing, but eventually life in San Moreno returned almost to normal.

Bill Martin figured there would always be some degree of tension in San Moreno, just like there was anywhere people with different backgrounds and views coexist. *Heck, wasn't that the classic American story?* Americans prided themselves on living in a melting pot, one that slowly assimilated all the different people who managed to find their way to its shore. *We're a nation of immigrants,* Martin reminded himself. He was just embarrassed it had taken almost losing his son to remember this most basic of civic lessons.

Personally, he believed that everyone in San Moreno had become a little closer and more friendly since Judge Lawson's verdict on the baseball cards had been announced. *People appreciate compromise. And even the youngest among us know fairness when they see it.*

Martin looked up the street and saw Tomás and Tommy laughing—surrounded by a dozen teenage girls. *Well that's interesting and probably to be expected.* Both boys were intelligent, funny, and kind—a catch for any girl. The fact that they were six years away from being millionaires and every girl within a hundred miles knew it only increased their appeal.

The baseball card auction had ended three days after the court hearing. An anonymous buyer purchased the cards for a little more than $63 million. Martin still had a hard time believing it: $63 million dollars. Judge Lawson had called a special conference to discuss how to distribute the "extra" $13 million dollars. The largest part—$10 million—was added to the $35 million already in the special San Moreno Trust Fund.

It had only been two weeks, but already the fund's trustees had agreed to one expenditure. The committee had allocated one million dollars to establish language classes at a nearby community college. Through the new program, Hispanic residents could learn English for free, and non-Hispanic residents could learn Spanish—also for free. Community leaders had come to realize that one of the biggest factors in the town's racial tension had been the inability for the two "sides" to communicate. Neither could, literally, understand the other.

Martin glanced back at the stage, where the legendary Texas rockers had now been joined by a fourth person. The sounds of "Sharp Dressed Man" blared across the town square. Bill Martin looked closer and saw that the fourth figure, wearing khaki shorts, sandals, and a floppy Panama Jack hat, was none other than Sam Coberly himself.

It had been Coberly who first suggested getting ZZ Top to perform at the festival. He had been a fan of the band for years and said he would "give a million dollars" to have the chance to meet the band. When he found out it wouldn't cost anywhere near a million dollars to get the band to perform, he quickly volunteered to pay for their appearance out of his share of the baseball card money.

Martin waved to get Tommy's attention, motioning for the two boys to follow him to his pickup.

*****

A half-hour later, Martin pulled his red pickup into a parking space in front of the old Five & Dime building. They were two blocks away from the celebration, and could still hear the booming music. Martin grabbed a flashlight with his good hand and climbed out of the pickup while Tomás and Tommy slid out on the passenger side.

At that exact moment Tomás's father pulled in beside Martin's truck.

"What's my dad doing here?" asked Tomás.

"Heck what are we doing here, Dad," Tommy chimed in. "We're missing the festival."

"Just be patient youngins. All in good time."

Bill Martin nodded as José joined them, then reached into his pocket for a set of old keys. He stepped forward and put his hand on the front door of the old Five & Dime.

"We'll just be a little bit," he told his son, sliding the key into the lock. "Thanks for coming, José."

"Happy to oblige," José replied.

Both fathers could tell their sons were more confused than ever—it was written all over their faces. Bill decided to put the boys out of their misery. "They're coming to tear down the old building first thing Monday, and I needed some help with something before they do. If that's okay with you and Tomás, Tommy? It will just take a minute."

Two quick nods gave Bill the answer he was looking for, as the foursome entered the building. Bill headed to the main checkout counter. He stepped behind it and aimed his flashlight at the hole in the wall where the baseball cards had been hidden.

"Dad, what are we looking for?" Tommy asked.

Bill didn't answer, but he and José exchanged a quick grin. Before Tommy could ask him again, Bill reached into his pocket and removed a crumpled sheet of paper, brown and dusty from age. He handed the paper to Tommy.

"What's this?" Tommy asked.

Tomás leaned in close to examine the faded writing. "Looks like some kind of old receipt," Tomás said.

"It's an invoice from 1952," Bill Martin said. "It's the original invoice for those cases of baseball cards you found."

Tomás looked up in surprise. "Really?" he said. "This is the actual receipt for those old cards?"

Bill Martin nodded. "It's from the Topps Company; the original invoice from when my father bought the cards sixty years ago. That's his signature at the bottom."

"Cool! Where did you find it?" Tommy asked.

Bill Martin pointed to the hole in the wall behind the counter. "I found it in there a couple of days after Tomás found the cards. I came down here to see where the cards had been hidden, and I saw a crumpled piece of paper lying back in the far corner. I didn't think anything of it at the time, but the next time I was in here I pulled it out and realized it was a receipt, a receipt for the cards."

Bill Martin turned his attention back to the room and once again shined his flashlight along the walls.

"Mr. Martin, with the wrecking crew coming Monday, do you need my dad and I to help you get that old counter out of here? If you do, I think we'll need a crowbar."

Before Bill could respond, Tommy grabbed his sleeve.

"Hey, Dad!" Tommy shouted. "Look at this!"

Bill Martin turned toward his son, a smile spreading across his face.

"I wondered how long it was going to take you to figure it out," he said.

Tomás looked confused. "Figure out what?" he asked.

Tommy held up the paper for Tomás to see.

"Look at the bottom," Tommy said. "See where it shows the total price paid?"

Tomás eyes glanced at the number. "Okay."

"Now," Tommy said. "Look at the same line on the other side, to the left."

Tomás's eyes moved across the page. "Okay."

"What does it say?"

"It says '10,' " Tomás answered.

"That's right," Tommy said excitedly. "Ten!"

Tomás still looked confused. Tommy rolled his eyes, growing impatient. "Don't you get it?"

"Apparently not," Tomás said.

"Ten is how many packages were ordered and delivered from the company," Tommy said.

You could almost see the wheels turning in Tomás's brain. "You mean your grandfather ordered and should have received ten cases of cards?" Tomás said.

"Exactly!" Tommy said.

"But I only found six," Tomás said.

"Exactly!" Tommy shouted even louder.

Tomás's eyes grew wide. "You mean . . ."

". . . either Grandpa sold some of the cards or there could be four more cases of those old cards still hidden here somewhere," Tommy said, his eyes darting around the building for potential hiding places.

Bill Martin stepped back outside to the pickup and returned a moment later with two more flashlights. José pulled another out of his back pocket. Bill looked first at Tommy and then at Tomás. "Shall we?" he said. "I don't know about you guys, but José and I would like to see if there is any more treasure hidden in this old store. And if there is, then we'll split whatever it is four ways. Deal?"

Tomás looked at his father and then Mr. Martin with a huge smile on his face, a smile bigger than the one Tommy had seen in the courtroom that fateful day not so long ago.

So this is what it's like to have family friends, Tomás thought. *I see now why they say good friends are better than gold. We may or may not find more treasure today but either way we will all leave here richer . . .*

Tommy gave his best friend a thumbs-up.

"Will you do the honors, José," Bill asked. "This cast still has me a little out of commission."

"It would be my pleasure," José said.

And as the two boys and Bill watched, José Martinez set aside his flashlight, stepped toward the wall, and grabbed the next section of wood paneling . . . and pulled.

He stepped back.

A gap was exposed in the wall, just like the one where Tomás had found the original stash of cards.

Bill Martin stepped up. His hands shook as he shined his flashlight deep into the opening, and both boys gasped at what they saw . . .

About the Author

Roy Deering is a middle school English teacher and a lifelong baseball fan and card collector. Before becoming a teacher, he spent more than twenty years as a journalist. He is married to his high school sweetheart, Beverly, and they have three children—two sons, Noah and Caleb, and a daughter, Grace. When Deering isn't writing, you can often find him exploring one of America's national parks or preaching for the Church of Christ. Roy makes his home in Oklahoma. Visit him at RoyDeering.com.